TRAIL BOSS FROM TEXAS

On his first night in the Timberlake Country, Larry Brennan fought in a street brawl with a young tough, discovered a corpse in his hotel room, struggled frantically in the dark for his Colt .45 and found himself accused of murder.

Brennan had come to Timberlake to deliver six hundred head of cattle to Jeff Halliday, only to find Halliday clubbed to death, and Halliday's nephew the prime murder suspect.

Caught in the killing crossfire between ranchers and unscrupulous land barons, Brennan made a desperate bid to save the Halliday ranch and future of the whole valley.

Peter B. Germano was born the oldest of six children in New Bedford, Massachusetts. During the Great Depression, he had to go to work before completing high school. It left him with a powerful drive to continue his formal education later in life, finally earning a Master's degree from Loyola University in Los Angeles in 1970. He sold his first Western story to A.A. Wyn's Ace Publishing magazine group when he was twenty years old. In the same issue of *Sure-Fire Western* (1/39) Germano had two stories, one by Peter Germano and the other by **Barry Cord**. He came to prefer the Barry Cord name for his Western fiction. When the Second World War came, he joined the U.S. Marine Corps. Following the war he would be called back to active duty, again as a combat correspondent, during the Korean conflict. In 1948 Germano began publishing a series of Western novels as Barry Cord, notable for their complex plots while the scenes themselves are simply set, with a minimum of description and quick character sketches employed to establish a wide assortment of very different personalities. The pacing, which often seems swift due to the adept use of a parallel plot structure (narrating a story from several different viewpoints), is combined in these novels with atmospheric descriptions of weather and terrain. *Dry Range* (1955), *The Sagebrush Kid* (1954), *The Iron Trail Killers* (1960), and *Trouble in Peaceful Valley* (1968) are among his best Westerns. "The great southwest . . ." Germano wrote in 1982, "this is the country, and these are the people that gripped my imagination . . . and this is what I have been writing about for forty years. And until I die I shall remain the little New England boy who fell in love with the 'West,' and as a man had the opportunity to see it and live in it."

TRAIL BOSS FROM TEXAS

Barry Cord

GUNSMOKE

First published in the UK by Foulsham

This hardback edition 2005
by BBC Audiobooks Ltd
by arrangement with
Golden West Literary Agency

ISBN 1 4056 8046 6

British Library Cataloguing in Publication Data available.

Printed and bound in Great Britain by
Antony Rowe Ltd., Chippenham, Wiltshire

Larry Brennan turned the roan against the driving rain and crossed Douglas' muddy street to the small rectangle of light painting the mud in front of the Timberlake Stables.

This was the end of a thousand-mile trail, but the fact did not lighten the Texan's weariness nor rid him of a nagging irritation that made him taut-nerved and surly. It had been as rough a drive as he had ever bossed, and the thought of Duke and the boys making the best of a wet camp did not please him.

The roan stopped in front of the barn and Larry leaned over the saddle horn and called: "Hello, in there!"

A stumpy figure with a thin face and a black patch over his right eye showed up in the crack and studied the Texan. The man muttered something unintelligible. Then the barn door creaked back on overhead runners, allowing Larry to ride inside.

A lantern sat on a big packing case, throwing a smoky yellow light over cards spread for solitaire. The strong smell of manure was sharp in the steamy heat that washed against Larry. The rain rattled noisily on the high-beamed roof and a horse stamped restlessly in one of the stalls.

Larry dismounted. The hostler slid the door back to within a yard of closing, then turned, and shuffled up to the Texan. "Helluva night, ain't it, stranger? You come in along the river trail?"

Larry said: "No," discouraging further gossip with the monosyllable. "Grain feed her an' bed her down," he instructed briefly. "I'll be around in the mornin'."

The hostler shrugged and picked up his lantern. Larry followed the stumpy man to a rear stall and helped him strip saddle and gear from the roan. "I'll take my warbag," he said as the hostler started to stuff it into a wall rack.

He slid the roll down near his feet and leaned back against the boards, unbuttoning his slicker to reach into his coat for the makings.

He was a big man, broad and compactly built, and there was a quiet sureness in his movements. He had put on a

5

clean shirt and a worn gray coat to come to town and the skirt of the coat hid the plain walnut butt of a Colt tied low on his right hip.

He lighted the cigarette, cupping the match in a rope-roughened palm, and with the first drag he felt weariness weigh him down, like a cement block settling on his broad shoulders.

He waited until the hostler finished. The stumpy man came out of the stall and picked up his lantern, and Larry said: "Where do I find the El Dorado?"

"Down the road a piece," the other said. He walked to the stable door where rain was making inroads through the small opening, and waved into the night. "Across the street an' to yore left. Can't miss it. Big, two-story buildin' with a false front an' a big board sign."

Larry came up beside him and started to unbutton his slicker. They both drew back as a rider suddenly loomed up out of the darkness.

The man said: "Open up, Ned."

Ned pushed the sliding door back and the man rode in and dismounted. The stableman slid the door back against the rain and turned to the newcomer.

"Howdy, Mister Allison."

"Hello, Ned." The man had a soft voice, like a woman's. "Take care of Nig for me."

"I sure will," Ned said. He ran a hand over the magnificent black's steaming flank. "Looks like you rode him pretty hard—"

"I was in a hurry," Allison said shortly. He unbuttoned his wet slicker and reached into his coat pocket for a ready-made cigarette. He glanced at Larry. "Lousy night to be on trail," he observed. "Coming or leaving our town?"

Larry turned. Ned had gone to the rear of the barn with the black and taken the lantern with him. The man he had addressed as Allison was a vague figure in the semi-darkness.

"Coming," he said shortly.

A match crackled on Allison's thumbnail. The flame lifted to the cigarette between his lips.

Larry had a glimpse of a lean, handsome face, close-shaved and well groomed—a touch of gray at the temples. The man puffed deeply and his eyes sought Larry's briefly before he blew the flame out.

Ned came back, swinging the light. "Did you hear about Halliday gettin' killed, Allison?"

"No." Allison turned and looked at Ned, and there was surprise in his glance. "No—I didn't hear. How'd it happen?"

Larry had been about to go out. He stopped, and started

6

to pull his slicker collar up around his ears, interest holding him in the doorway.

"Found him clubbed to death in the El Dorado about an hour ago," the hostler said. "Velie, the night clerk, found him lyin' on the floor by the bed..."

"Who killed him?"

Ned shrugged. "Velie says it must have been Bob Masters. That's what he told Albright. Claims Bob was up in Halliday's room a couple of hours earlier an' he could hear them arguin' clear down into the lobby. When Masters came downstairs he had a cut on his lip. That's what started Velie to thinkin'—an' after a while he went upstairs to see if Halliday was all right...."

Allison frowned. The garrulous stableman fumbled in his unbuttoned vest for the remnants of his plug and popped it into his mouth. "Looks like the case of bitin' the hand that fed him," he said indistinctly. "That Masters kid is sure a wild one."

A hard smile flickered across Allison's face. "Yeah—too wild." He glanced at Larry. The Texan was standing by the opening, staring into the rain, finishing his cigarette.

"What's McVail doing about it?"

"Nothin'. The sheriff's outta town. An' Albright ain't made a move to pick up the kid, though he's in town somewhere. So's his sister."

Allison ground his cigarette out under his heel. "Well, that's the law's problem," he said indifferently. He walked to the door and paused briefly at Larry's side. "Hope you like our town, stranger," he said politely, and stepped out into the rain.

Larry took a last puff on his cigarette and snapped it out into the trampled mud. Ned came up beside him and stared after Allison's striding figure. "That's Charley Allison," he said. "Owns the Ace of Spades outfit down the valley an' the Casino in town. Doesn't look it—but Charley's a bad man to get into an argument with."

"I wouldn't have guessed it," Larry said shortly, unimpressed. The shock of Halliday's death was still strong. Turning, he sought confirmation by a casual remark. "I used to know a man named Halliday. Ran into him down in Texas a couple of years ago. Wonder if it might be the same man you just mentioned."

The stumpy man took the bait. "Not this Halliday. Jeff hasn't been out of Timberlake valley since he came into it near thirty years ago."

Larry stood in the doorway, not seeing the wet street of

7

the strange town a thousand miles from his Texas starting point. His feet were wet inside his scuffed boots and he felt chill and uncomfortable and a little disheartened.

He had over six hundred head of cattle and eight men standing guard over them half a day's ride out of town. Cows for Jeff Halliday!

The rain rattled noisily on the roof and the Texan thought of the long trail miles, the treacherous river crossings, the dry stretches and the cold he and his men had endured. And now Halliday was dead and Larry had on his hands a herd badly in need of pasturage.

He felt the stableman's curious stare and shook off the wearying thoughts. "Too bad about Halliday," he said. "Hope nobody takes a fancy to try the same with me." He picked up his roll. "See yuh in the mornin'."

The rain hit him like birdshot, driving into his face. He ducked his head against it and cut across the street, hating the ankle-deep mud that sucked at his boots.

He reached the boardwalk and swung left, following Ned's directions. It was not late, but the storm kept the inhabitants of the trail town indoors. The Texan strode down the walk, his heels making a flat sound on the boards. The wooden awning there extended to the street and it sheltered him from the downpour.

Halfway down the block he paused, dropped his bag, and rolled a cigarette. The smoke felt good in his lungs. He relaxed against a darkened door and tried to think.

A couple of horsemen rode past, hunched against the rain. They turned a corner and left the road deserted except for a buckboard tied up at the end of the block.

The wind had its way tonight, gusting noisily against the dark buildings, and the rain pelting the puddles had a dreary sound.

A thousand miles. The thought went through him flatly, leaving a bitter taste in his mouth. A thousand miles for nothing.

He finished his cigarette and picked up his bag.

A girl came out on the walk, pulling the collar of her raincoat up around her neck. The wind came around the corner, buffeting her as she climbed into the buckboard. The team moved restlessly as she gathered up the reins.

The Texan felt her quick glance as he drew abreast of the buckboard. She was stiff against the driving rain, her face in shadow—and he felt impatience in her.

She was evidently waiting for the man who came out of the lighted doorway just ahead of the Texan. He stepped

8

out without warning and Larry instinctively thrust a hand forward to fend off a collision.

The man jumped like a startled cat at the touch of the Texan's hand. He whirled and crouched, his voice lashing out at Larry in bitter challenge. "Keep yore hands off me, damn you!"

He was a youngster barely topping twenty— a lithe, cat-wiry kid with a mop of yellow hair and a bitter, tight-lipped face.

He was jumpy—and dangerous. In the split second that followed the Texan sensed this. It should have made him cautious, but he was in a surly mood and now anger ran quickly through him, flattening his voice.

"Get out of my way!"

The girl's voice cut in sharply behind him. "Bob! Don't start any trouble. . . ."

Larry was stepping past the youngster, brushing him contemptuously aside. The kid whirled like a striking cat. His fingers closed on Larry's shoulder; he pulled the big Texan around and slapped his face. His voice was low and intense. "What's the matter, big boy? Haven't yuh got the guts—"

The kid's tone, more than the slap, drew violence from Brennan. His bag was in his right hand—he dropped it as he clamped his left around the youngster's gun wrist. He used his shoulder and his weight to jam his squirming assailant against the building and his powerful hand twisted until the kid's fingers unclenched and his gun dropped to the walk.

Larry stepped back and slapped the youngster's face, cuffing him with a series of blows that furnished an outlet for his raw anger.

The girl had said something he had not understood in the first burst of his anger, but now her voice was close and sharp, striking into his awareness.

"Quit it, stranger! And don't make a move for your gun!"

Larry shoved the youngster roughly against the wall, kicked his Colt out of reach, and turned.

The girl was standing just behind him, vague in the shadows. The nickel-plated revolver in her gauntleted hand reflected light in tiny wet beads along its barrel.

The youngster was backed against the building, shaking his head. He looked like some wild animal who had been clubbed and was ready to spring.

Anger simmered in Larry. "You his keeper, ma'am?"

"Yes," she said. There was a contempt in her that drew his ire, an antagonism at once definite and unexplained.

"Then take him home before he gets hurt."

9

The kid lunged away from the wall. Larry turned, but the girl was between them, the revolver leveled at a spot just above the Texan's belt.

"There'll be no more trouble tonight!" she said harshly. "Bob, get up on the buckboard. We've got a long way to go."

The youngster caught himself with an effort. He looked past her to Larry, and a streak of light from within the building touched the lean, taut lines of his jaw. A muscle quivered in his cheek. Then he stepped back, retrieved his Colt, and walked to the buckboard.

Larry's shoulders prickled, but he did not look around. The slim girl glanced at him contemptuously. "Next time you try to do a job for Allison wait until our backs are turned. Or use the darkness of an alley!"

The rain pattered swiftly along the top of the awning as she stepped back and climbed into the seat beside her brother. The restless team swung away from the hitchrack and went trotting up the street. The girl and the boy didn't look back.

The anger died slowly in Larry, leaving a flat residue of wonder. A strange pair. And then, thinking he would not be long in Douglas, he dismissed them. He was starting for the El Dorado, the sign of which he could see across the side street, when a voice said: "You're the first man I saw do it, stranger. Manhandle Bob Masters!"

Chapter 2

Dead Man's Room

Larry turned. A spare-framed character in a long black coat and a stovepipe hat stood in the doorway. The light was behind him, silhouetting his indolent figure, and Larry frowned, sensing more than a casual interest in the man's voice.

"Good thing his sister was along," the character continued. He spoke as if he had something in his mouth. He shifted a little and the light outlined the left side of his seamed face, bringing into view a corncob pipe. "Yep," he repeated. "Lucky fer you his sister was along. Lennie Masters is the only person who kin handle him."

"A bad hombre, eh?" Larry said. Then his eyes picked up the rifle the man had placed by his side against the

10

door framing, and suddenly he knew how close he had come to death.

"For a wild kid he seems to have a lot of friends," Larry said tightly. His glance moved from the faintly smiling man to gilt lettering on the show windows behind him: *Sam Luce, Undertaker*.

"I'm Luce," the man said quietly. "Some people call me Socrates Sam—on account I ask a lot of questions."

He watched Larry shift his bag to his other hand. "You ride for Charley Allison?"

The rain pounded fast and thin on the awning and tiredness came back to the big Texan. He was in no mood for this sort of conversational fencing.

"No," he said curtly, and turned away.

"Wait."

Larry frowned and looked back.

"It was a fair question," the undertaker said.

"Look," Larry said flatly. "I'm a stranger here. Rode in less than fifteen minutes ago, looking for a man named Jeff Halliday—"

"You came late," Sam said. He straightened and knocked his pipe against the framing. "Come inside. I'll show you what's left of Jeff."

Larry hesitated. He felt empty inside, as if all purpose had been drained out of him. Halliday had meant nothing to him and he didn't fancy looking at a corpse, but he followed the undertaker inside.

The front room, serving as a waiting room for the relatives of the deceased, had stuffed horsehair furniture and the faint smell of flowers and death. Sam opened a rear door that led into his workshop where he did his embalming.

A body lay on a plain wooden table, covered by a shroud. The undertaker beckoned Larry to him and when the Texan was at his side, he raised a corner of the shroud.

Larry glanced at the features of a leathery-faced man in his fifties. Then Sam dropped the shroud and Larry stepped back and rolled a cigarette.

The smell of death and chemicals in the room sickened him. He drew in a lungful of smoke and looked at Sam. "I heard Halliday was clubbed to death."

Sam nodded. He dipped his pipe into an oil-skin pouch and thumbed tobacco into the corncob. "Jeff was killed in his room at the El Dorado a little over an hour ago. His nephew, Bob Masters, was the last man to see him alive."

Larry frowned. "Nephew?"

"You'll hear talk that Bob killed his uncle in a quarrel,"

11

Sam said. He scraped a match on the seat of his pants and touched the flame to his pipe. "Bob's a wild one," he admitted, puffing deeply. "But he didn't kill Jeff."

Larry was silent.

"Jeff was a close friend of mine," the undertaker added. "We came into the valley together when Douglas was a crossroads town an' elk grazed over range now owned by the Tumblin' H an' the Ace of Spades."

He paused and looked at Larry as if wondering how far he should go. The Texan waited, letting him make his own decision.

"There's a fight on now for control of the valley," Sam finally said. "Allison's makin' his bid for it. He owns the Ace of Spades across the river from the Tumblin' H. In the past months some pretty hard characters have been passin' through town, goin' up to join his outfit."

Larry shrugged and Sam dropped his eyes to the gun bulging against Larry's slicker.

"Bob Masters took you for one of them just now," he said.

"It makes sense," the Texan admitted. And then, because he had his own problem, he asked: "Who's runin' the Tumblin' H now?"

"Jeff was a bachelor," Sam replied. "Bob an' Lennie Masters have been with him since they were toddlers an' they're all the relatives he had. They'll be takin' over the Tumblin' H an' tryin' to run it, with the help of Bill Tate, Halliday's old foreman."

The rain made a lonely sound on the roof and suddenly Larry was acutely conscious of it.

"Too bad," he said dryly. He turned and walked out of the room.

Sam followed him to the outside door. "The Tumblin' H is nearly shot to hell," he said, as if it should mean something to the Texan. "Jeff was tryin' to keep it together until he got help from a friend of his in Texas."

Larry frowned. "Well?"

Sam looked at him. "You the Texan Jeff was expectin'?"

"Yeah," Larry said shortly. "It looks like I got here too late."

He turned and left Sam staring after him.

The sign creaked dismally over El Dorado's door as Larry passed below it. Out of the rain, he loosened his slicker and shook water from his battered Stetson.

There was no one in the small lobby except the night clerk at the desk. A pair of potted palms graced the center of the room. There was a dining room off to the left, closed now, and up by the stairs slatted doors testified to a hotel bar. Voices and the click of glasses came to the tired Texan as he walked to the counter.

The clerk was a keen-faced young man with a wisp of blond mustache and a sour twist to his lips. He glanced up as Larry paused at the desk and nodded none too graciously. "Yeah—we got a room. Just been vacated." He turned a well thumbed register around and handed Larry a stubby pencil.

Larry signed. He turned and looked at the bar, but decided he was too tired even for a drink.

The clerk was looking down at the register when he asked: "There a telegraph office in town?"

"On Lodestone Avenue," the clerk replied. "Two blocks south." He glanced up at the wall clock ticking under dusty elk antlers over the bar entrance.

"You're too late to send a message tonight. Jake closes at ten."

Larry said: "It can wait." He picked up his bag. "Does a key go with the room?"

"I'll show you where it is," the clerk said. He came out from behind the desk, limping a little. "Sorry I have to do it, Mister Brennan."

"Do what?"

"Give you this room. A man was killed in it a while ago."

Larry paused and the clerk looked back. He wet his lips. "It's the only thing we have right at this moment—"

"It's all right," Larry said, "long as the bed's clean."

The room in which Halliday had been killed was at the rear of a long narrow hall. A window in the end wall opened to back stairs. Rain rattled against the streaked panes.

The clerk opened the door with a key, stepped inside and scraped a match. He lighted the lamp in a wall bracket by the door, placed the long key with its hotel tag on the bedside table and looked at Larry.

Brennan said: "It'll do," and frowned as the man limped hurriedly out and went downstairs.

He looked at the iron-framed bed, the scarred dresser, the worn rug and the cheap print of a buffalo hunt on one wall and the Lincoln portrait on the other.

He was very tired. The bed was inviting, and a cynical mood thrust off the slight repulsion that came to him at the thought of Halliday's death.

Peeling off his slicker, he dropped it over a chair back. His coat was next. Rain had seeped down his neck and wet his blue cotton shirt in streaks across his wide shoulders.

13

Still frowning, he walked to the bed and sat down. The springs creaked dismally.

Unconsciously he reached into his shirt pocket for the letter he had carried with him from Texas. It was to have been his identification to Halliday. Terse and to the point, it did not explain why Jeff had been in trouble, or indicate who might have killed him.

It was addressed to John Barstow of the Triangle spread, and read:

> *Dear John:*
> *It's been a long time since you were up this way. Things are not going so well with me. Being forced to sell or get out, and I don't want to sell and am too old to move.*
> *Need five hundred head of grazing stock by the end of September or I go under. Can you help me out?*

It was signed: *Your old trailmate, Jeff Halliday.* The letter was written in a woman's fine hand, but the signature was evidently Jeff's. There was a P. S. and a roughly drawn map of the Timberlake country. The P.S. contained instructions for the Triangle trail boss to leave the herd in the canyon marked X on the map, then to come to town and get a room in El Dorado where Halliday would get in touch with him.

Brennan scowled as he repocketed the letter. He had obeyed instructions. He had left Duke Sayer in charge of the Triangle herd, with orders to take things easy until he got back. He had come to Douglas expecting to find Halliday and to arrange delivery of the cattle.

Now it didn't seem so simple.

He stood up and unbuckled his gun belt. He hung it over the bed post so that the plain walnut butt of the heavy .45 dangled near the pillow. Walking to the wall light, he blew out the flame. He turned and stood a moment, looking at the black-streaked window, thinking of the boys huddled in a wet camp.

His orders had been to deliver the herd to Jeff Halliday —and Halliday was dead. He didn't relish the drive back to the Triangle.

He walked to the window and looked out onto the back stairs that led to the yard. Rain tapped on the glass. It was Barstow's problem, he thought, but it annoyed him. He'd have to wire the Triangle boss in the morning, explain what had happened, and wait for an answer.

Standing there, he recalled the look on Barstow's face the

14

day the Triangle owner had called Larry into the ranch-house. The old rancher had handed Larry the letter from Halliday and waited until Larry finished reading it.

"Been a long time since I had a drink with Jeff," the old man had said quietly. "Looks like he's in trouble. Cut out six hundred head that kin stand the drive. Pick yore own crew. Help Jeff out."

Well, it was too late to help Halliday.

The Texan walked back to the bed and pulled off his boots. The bed creaked as he stretched his big frame on the cover. He placed both hands under his head and stared up at the dark ceiling.

Finally he slept.

The rain was still drumming against the window when the Texan's eyes snapped open. The room was a pit of darkness. Nothing moved within its confines. But Larry lay quiet, alert, knowing something had awakened him.

For a long minute he lay still, listening to the storm brawl against the building. Then, as he turned and reached up for his Colt, he heard a sound.

Someone was fumbling with the knob.

Larry whipped his stockinged feet over the bedside and straightened to sitting position. He lifted his gun from its holster and crossed the room to the wall beside the door.

In the hallway a voice breathed: "Jeff—" and cut off, as if the man were suddenly out of breath.

Larry frowned. He shifted his grip on the Colt, holding it flat in his hand and bringing it up by his ear for a quick, chopping stroke.

The knob turned. The door swung inward. Larry shifted his position as a shadowy figure lurched into the room, hit the door with his shoulder, and sprawled on his face.

The door banged against the other wall and jarred back against the man on the floor.

Larry lowered his Colt. He waited, puzzled and tense. No one seemed to have heard the commotion. He could hear men talking in the bar off the lobby—the voices drifted faint-ly up the stairs. In the room across the hall a man snored loudly.

Larry bent over his uninvited guest. His eyes were becom-ing adjusted to the darkness and a diffusion of light from downstairs dimly lighted the sprawled figure. The man was short and wiry and his patched, misshapen clothes were wet and clung to his thin frame like wet wallpaper.

Larry knelt beside him. The man was hurt—he was sprawled on his face, his hands clenching and unclenching

15

with spasms of pain. Larry turned him over and lifted him to a sitting position. The man sagged against his arm, his head lolling back, "Jeff—damn—I got it. In my pocket..."

His voice choked off into a gasp. He looked up at Larry, not seeing him. He had a thin, pinched face covered with pinpoints of white beard. He looked like some drunken bum. But he was dying—and he thought he was speaking to Jeff Halliday.

Larry said: "I'm not—" and stopped, knowing his explanation would not matter.

"You won't have to pay me—Jeff. Won't do me any good—now. Saber caught me goin' through—" His breath whistled as he labored to finish. "Knifed me— but I got away—" He stiffened, straining hard against Larry's arm— then he relaxed. . . .

Larry didn't move right away. He stood there, a dead man in his arms, listening to the rain. Evidently no one had seen this man come up through the lobby—or if so, had not given it any thought.

Whoever he was, the man had not known Jeff Halliday was dead. And he had come to Halliday's room to deliver something for which Halliday had been willing to pay.

Larry tossed his Colt on the bed and eased the body back on the floor. He reached into the dead man's pocket, found nothing and was fumbling inside the other when a board creaked in the hallway just outside the door.

A voice whispered softly: "Don't move! Don't even turn around!"

Larry didn't move.

He heard another floor board creak, and the faint jingle of spurs. Then someone loomed over him. A pair of scuffed muddy boots paused close beside him. Larry could see black-striped pants tucked into the boot tops, noted that one steel spur had the rowel missing.

There was an instant of silence, then one of the boots moved, and the thought flashed through the Texan that the man standing over him was raising his Colt for a clubbing blow.

The scalp above Larry's ears prickled, gambling that his assailant would not risk a shot, Larry suddenly lunged side-wise, slamming his weight against the other's knees.

The man cursed as he took a header over the Texan.

Larry scrambled to his feet. Inside the room his assailant was doing the same. His silhouette showed briefly against the window and Larry plunged toward him, driving his shoulder into the man. They went back onto the bed and Larry got his hand on the man's throat.

16

The prowler drove a hard knee into Larry's stomach. The Texan grunted and the other twisted violently, breaking Larry's hold. Larry made a lunge for the man as he broke away from the bed—his fingers closed on the man's shoulder and he felt cloth tear in his hand as the man lunged free.

A fist drove into Larry's face, throwing him off balance. Losing the man in the darkness, Larry turned and made a dive for the bed where he had so carelessly tossed his Colt a few minutes before.

A .45 roared, its jarring report filling the room with noise. The slug ripped into the bedding beside Larry. Then the Texan was rolling over into the small area between the bed and the far wall, carrying his Colt with him.

Spurs jingled thinly. Larry came erect in time to catch a glimpse of a vague figure vanishing through the doorway. Hurdling the bed, Larry reached the door and stared blankly down an empty hallway.

Shouts were coming up from the lobby. A door midway down the hall opened slowly and a whiskered, sleepy-eyed man cautiously looked out. The Texan turned and went back inside the room. He closed the door and bent by the dead man, his fingers reaching inside the wet coat pocket.

He found a long white envelope, containing a letter. It was too dark to read, to find out what it meant. But he had no doubt that the man at his feet had been killed because of this, and that Jeff Halliday had been willing to pay money for it.

He straightened, suddenly aware that men were tramping up the steps. Crossing to the bed, he slipped his Colt into its holster and the envelope inside his coat pocket.

Then he sat on the bed and waited for developments.

Chapter 3

The Stranger Can Wait!

There was confusion in the hallway. Someone yelled: "Where was the shootin'?" A door opened and voices asked questions. Boots tramped toward Brennan's door. Someone opened it and called loudly: "Hey! You hear the shootin'?" Larry did not answer, and the slightly tipsy intruder took a step forward into the dark room. "Hey! Wake up—"

He tripped over the dead man and fell on his hands and knees. *"Kee-ripes!"* he growled, staggering to his feet. "Al-

17

bright!" He walked to the door and yelled down the hall. "Hey! Albright! There's a dead man in here!"

Boots clumped down the hall and into the room. Someone stumbled over the body and cursed. Someone else scraped a match. A hard, horsy face looked at Larry above the match flame. Then the light was carried to the bracketed oil lamp and the yellow glare revealed half a dozen men crowding around in the room and the hallways just outside the door.

Larry slipped into his boots. "Looks like guest night," he said, and then, holding his gaze on the lanky man who had struck the match, he added: "I don't know the man, Deputy, an' I don't know how it happened."

The deputy gave him a hard look as he knelt beside the victim. "Bates!" he said in a surprised voice. "It's old Whiskey Bates—"

"Yeah—an' knifed in the back," an onlooker added, turning hostile eyes to Larry. "I ain't never cared for the ol' bum, Ben—but even Bates deserved an even break!"

"Knifed?" another voice said. "What the hell was the shot we heard?"

The deputy made no comment. He got up and walked to the head of the bed and drew out Larry's Colt. He was a lanky individual with a taciturn expression and straw hair. A stub of a cigar, unlighted, jutted from his tight lips.

Some wit had made the classic remark that Ben Albright would wind up stoking a furnace down below still chewing on the same cigar stub.

He checked the loads in Larry's Colt, sniffed at the muzzle. Then he replaced the weapon and looked impassively at the Texan.

"All right," he said out of the corner of his mouth. "How'd it happen?"

"I don't know," Larry said.

The deputy frowned. He turned and went back to Bates and looked down at him. The long rip in the dead man's coat was dark with blood. He stood staring down at the body, then turned, his voice striking out at the Texan.

"When'd you get in, stranger?"

Larry caught a glimpse of the night clerk hovering in the background. "About eleven," he answered. "Came upstairs an' fell asleep. Next thing I heard was a shot—then you came in."

He saw no reason to be more explicit, to explain how he had tangled with the man who had followed Bates to his room. There was too much going on in Douglas he didn't know about, and until he had more answers he was going to play his hand close to his chest.

18

The deputy scowled. "Kinda queer, ain't it, stranger, that a bum like Bates should pick your room to die in?"

Larry shrugged. "Ain't it?"

"Passin' through?"

Larry said: "Yeah—passin' through. Came in outta the rain an' took a room for the night. Can I help it if a man comes wanderin' in here in the middle of the night—"

"He must've had a reason, seein' as how he had a knife in his back when he started wanderin'," the deputy growled.

The man behind the deputy said: "Ain't this the room Jeff was killed in?" and Albright nodded. "Mebbe that's why Bates came up here," he said thoughtfully.

Albright stood by the wall, hard and scowling, and for a moment the patter of the rain was the only sound that broke the silence in the room. Then he said: "All right—one of you hombres give me a hand with the ol' man. We'll take him down to Socrates Sam."

Someone remarked a little sarcastically: "Sam's doin' a thrivin' business tonight, Ben." And the deputy looked at Larry and said: "Yeah—he's got his hands full."

He was in the doorway, holding the dead man under the arms, when he paused and looked back at Brennan. "I'll be seein' you in the mornin', stranger," he ordered harshly. "Don't try to leave town tonight."

The footsteps and the arguing voices died away down the hall. Larry crossed the room and closed the door. He stood looking at the bed, not listening to the monotonous beat of the rain against the window.

He was getting deeper into trouble without knowing why, and anger began to crawl through him, making him restless and impatient. He walked to the chair where he had tossed his coat and took the envelope from a pocket.

It had a Kansas Pacific stamped return address up in the left-hand corner, and it was addressed to Mark Carsons, First National Bank, Douglas, Colorado.

It read:

Dear Mark:
Surveyors will begin driving stakes for right of way through Timberlake Valley in the fall. Your original estimate of right of way correct.
Full details later.
                    Respectfully,
                              L. J. Jacobson.

Larry slipped the envelope back into his coat pocket and rolled a cigarette. He still didn't know what the situation

19

there was, except that the KP was building through the valley and someone had followed Bates to get that letter back. And Halliday had been willing to pay money for it.

He shrugged and walked to the door, propping a straight-backed chair against the knob. He was dog-tired, and someone might try to break in again. Larry had no wish to wind up at Socrates Sam's. He walked to the window and raised it. It was hard to lift and squealed going up. Rain whipped in against the faded curtains. Larry closed it and pulled down the shade.

Anyone trying to get in through the window would give ample warning.

The cigarette began to burn his fingers and he ground it out on the floor. There was nothing further he could do until he sent a wire to Barstow and got an answer.

The rain had given way to a cold drizzle when Larry awakened. Gray daylight seeped around the edges of the pulled-down blind. The room looked dingy and cold and Larry felt irritation pull at him, leaving him raw-nerved and unrefreshed.

He rolled out of bed, found water in a tin pitcher on the stand beside the dresser and poured it into the basin. He washed. Drying himself with a towel he found on a hook behind the door, he looked at himself in the dressing mirror.

His hair was black and shaggy on his sunburned neck. His face was broad and the bones of his cheeks stood out against the slightly hooked ridge of his nose. It was a hard face, not given to much idle laughter, but there were crinkles of humor around his blue-gray eyes. His torso was wide and solid and flat-muscled. He was a big man, packing two hundred pounds on a six-foot-one frame, but years in the saddle had kept him lean and long-muscled and he didn't look as if he weighed that much.

He was twenty-seven. He had been on his own since turning fourteen, and he had been in a lot of towns on both sides of the Mexican border. He had had his share of fiddlefooting and he was getting tired of it.

This was his last drive for the Triangle, he thought, and it pleased him. Let Barstow get himself another trail boss. He was ready to settle down.

He threw the towel on the dresser and ran his fingers through his beard. He needed a shave, he thought, and some bacon and eggs to ease the clamor in his stomach.

There was another clerk behind the desk when he came down into the lobby. An older man sitting with his feet up on the counter. He looked curiously at the Texan as he said: "Good morning, Mister Brennan."

Larry nodded briefly. The odor of frying bacon made his nostrils twitch, and he headed for the dining room on the opposite side of the lobby.

A scattering of customers were eating at tables. He felt their curious glances as he picked out a seat near the window. An elderly woman took his order, and as he waited, Larry looked idly into the muddy street.

The drizzle was like a gray mist, and the false fronts looked drab and dismal in the dull light. Horses nosed the rail of a saloon across the street, moving restlessly in fetlock-deep mud. A covered wagon, its six-horse team lunging in their traces, rolled by, headed for the gold fields further north.

Right now it was just a trail town, kept alive by the settlers and ranchers in the valley and fed by newcomers coming up the river trail. But Larry knew what would happen once news that the Kansas Pacific would be building through the valley reached the ears of Douglas. There would be a mad scramble for land—a score of new businesses would open their doors—and for every legitimate house would rise a false-fronted gambling house with hard-eyed men at roulette wheel and card table, ready to take money from the suckers.

Larry had seen rail towns before and he liked the thought that he would not be there when the boom hit Douglas. He lighted a cigarette and smoked until the waitress brought him a large order of bacon and potatoes and scrambled eggs.

He was spearing his last hashed-brown potato when the conversation of two men a few feet away intruded into his preoccupation.

"... Albright won't do a thing until Sheriff McVail gets back. But jailing's too good for that wild Masters kid. If Velie says he thinks Bob killed his uncle, I believe it. He should be made to stand trial—"

"I wouldn't want to be in McVail's place," the other man said. "Allison's been importing a bunch of hardcase gunslingers since the kid threatened to kill him on sight. The Ace of Spades is primed for trouble. And no telling what the Tumbling H is gonna do now—with Jeff dead. That leaves the Masterses in control and—" He glanced at Larry and dropped his voice.

Larry finished breakfast and lighted another cigarette. The impatience had gone out of him. There was trouble here— the conversation he had just overheard bore that out. But he was going to have none of it.

21

I'll send a wire to Barstow, and hang around, keeping out of trouble, until I get an answer. Ought to ride out and tell the boys the situation, though, he thought.

He got up, paid his check at the cashier's, and went out. He located a barbershop across the street, next door to a saloon. A swamper was wringing out a mop on the steps. He stopped and looked at Larry crossing the muddy road.

There was the customary red and white painted pole in front of the shop and *Tony's* painted in white letters across the show window. A customer was just vacating the single seat when Larry entered. The Texan hung his coat on the hook, shifted his gun belt, and walked to the chair.

Tony said: "Be right weeth you, *señor*. Sit down, please." He was counting money in a cigar box. Larry could see him in the big mirror as he settled back in the seat. A short, rolypoly, olive-skinned man with a brace of mustachios that curled up to his ears.

There was a hard step on the boardwalk. Then someone came into the shop.

Larry caught a glimpse of a tall, swarthy-faced man in the mirror as Tony turned and came up to him.

"Shave," Larry said. "An' you might as well trim some of this wool off my neck. I feel like Custer—"

"You're a little ahead of yourself, mister!" a voice said coldly. "I'm next."

Larry frowned and turned his head.

The newcomer was a rangy man with the dark, high-cheeked face of an Apache and the air of a man not used to being crossed. An expensively cut long gray coat reached well below his hips. Larry's cursory glance did not miss the bulge of a waist-high special holster under the coat.

The man was evidently looking for trouble. He took off his coat, hung it beside Larry's, and started for the chair. The long-barreled Colt .45 held by a clip holster, rode snug against his flowered waistcoat.

"Shave and trim, Tony," he said. He had a nasal, unpleasant voice. "The stranger can wait!"

Chapter 4

Keep Out Of Trouble, Brennan

Larry sat up. Tony had paused, his face whitening "*Si*, Meester Trellis—you are next." He looked at Brennan and spread his hands helplessly.

22

"Like hell you are!" Larry snapped. "Where I come from a man waits his turn, just like anyone else!"

Nick Trellis paused, obsidian black eyes studying the Texan. Then he took a step forward and closed long fingers in a fistful of Larry's shirt. "I said I'm next!" he sneered, and jerked Larry forward in the chair.

Larry came out of the chair under his own power, jerking free of Nick's grip.

Trellis had come looking for trouble, and he got it. Larry didn't give him a chance to go for his Colt.

Nick was stepping back, trying to get clear, when the big Texan sank a maul-like fist into the swarthy man's stomach. The breath went out of Nick with that one smash—and the fight as well. He doubled. Larry ducked under him and straightened, with Nick draped across his shoulder like a sack of oats. Taking three strides that took him to the front of the shop, the big Texan shifted his limp burden for better leverage and heaved him through the show window.

The glass showered down around Nick. He rolled limply to the edge of the walk and was prevented from going into the muddy street by a rain barrel standing under a wooden trough.

The jangling glass brought men from across the street and others along the boardwalk. Larry waited in front of the shattered window, a scowl on his beard-stubbled face, as the crowd gathered around Trellis.

Curious eyes glanced at him. Then someone with an officious voice said: "Better get him over to Doc Stillwell's before he bleeds to death."

Larry walked back to the chair and relaxed with his head against the head rest. "Forget about the window, Tony," he said. "I'll pay you for it."

Tony had been staring like a wax dummy by the chair. He came out of his trance and began to bob his head. *"Si, si, señor. Muy pronto."*

His hand shook as he whipped up lather in a mug and began to brush it on Larry's face. The Texan relaxed and listened to the jabber of voices outside.

"Sure—I saw it. Tossed Nick through the window, like he was a grain sack."

"Nick'll kill him!" another voice said. "Unless he leaves town in a hurry."

"Who is he, anyway?" someone asked. "One of Allison's new gunnies?"

"Naw," the first voice replied. "He wouldn't a tangled with Nick if he was. . . ."

The voice faded and there was a moment of silence. Then

23

boots sounded on the walk and scraped leisurely across the threshold of Tony's barbershop.

Tony stopped scraping the left side of Larry's face. He stood poised over the Texan, razor uplifted, looking uncertainly toward the door.

"For a stranger who hit town just last night, Brennan, you have a peculiar habit of gettin' into a heap of trouble."

Larry turned his head. He had heard that flat voice before.

Deputy Albright walked into the room and leaned his lanky frame against a shelf lined with shaving mugs. He was as tight-lipped and hard as he'd appeared the night before, and the same stub of cigar jutted from his lips. But there was a glint of suspicion in his eyes as he looked at Larry.

"I see you've been readin' the El Dorado register," Larry said, easing back in his chair.

"Yeah," Albright admitted easily. "Habit of mine." He shifted the cigar stub to the other side of his mouth and scratched his ear. "Been doin' a bit of checkin' up, too," he added.

"Yo're takin' that badge too seriously," Larry said. "Don't overwork it."

"Uh-huh," Albright glanced at the shattered window. He shook his head. "Nick Trellis is one of Douglas' more prominent citizens," he said. "In a dangerous way, I mean. Tossin' him through Tony's winder wasn't exactly polite."

Larry frowned. "You got somethin' on yore mind—beside your hat," he said. "All right, you talk—I'll listen. Tony, go ahead an' finish shavin' this bristle off my face."

Albright said: "Sure, I'll tell you what I know, an' then I'll speak my piece. First, you rode into town on a blaze-faced roan about ten last night. Good-lookin' animal with a Triangle brand not registered in these parts. You met Allison at the Timberlake stables, then asked about a man named Halliday. After that you headed for the El Dorado.

"You ran into Bob Masters an' his sister in front of Socrates Sam's," the deputy continued. "Had a bit of trouble with the Masterses. Then you got a room in the El Dorado. It happened to be the same room Jeff Halliday was killed in. Two hours after you turned in, there was a shot. I was down in the hotel bar. When we came upstairs we found Bates dead in yore room."

He was silent while Tony finished shaving Brennan. He looked out the window where broken glass littered the boardwalk. A couple of onlookers fidgeted under his direct stare and moved away.

Larry sat up.

"I told you what I knew about that last night," he said.

"No," Albright answered. He chewed thoughtfully on the cigar stub. "Not everythin', Brennan. I know Bates was knifed before he got to yore room. He was dyin' when he got there. Someone followed him an' took a shot at you."

He made a disparaging gesture with his hands as Larry said: "Yo're guessin', Deputy."

"I never guess," Albright said. "I was up in yore room this mornin', lookin' for you. Found where a slug had ripped into yore beddin'."

Larry shrugged. "All right," he admitted. "So someone followed Bates an' took a shot at me. He missed."

The deputy smiled faintly. "Sure," he said. "It's yore hide." His eyes narrowed suddenly and his voice struck out at Brennan, hard and decisive.

"You didn't say why you came to Douglas, Brennan, but I know. Yo're a Texan—it's on the hotel register. An' Halliday was expectin' help from Texas. Well, Halliday's dead. What do you intend doin'?"

Larry looked at him. "Nothin'," he said shortly, "until I get word from home."

Albright turned. He walked lazily to the door; then he stopped and looked back. "There's trouble ridin' the Timberlake ranges," he said sharply. "Keep yore riders out of it, Brennan!"

"Is that an order?"

The lawman nodded. "Yeah. There's too many hard characters struttin' around town as it is without a bunch of wild Texans mixin' things up. An' that goes double for you, Brennan, keep out of trouble while yo're in town!"

The Texan's eyes hardened, but he kept his voice level. "I don't make a habit of lookin' for it," he said coldly.

"That ain't enough!" the lawman snapped. *"Keep out of it!"* He turned and went out, kicking a sliver of glass into the mud as he crossed the street.

Tony finished cutting Larry's hair and brushed his neck and ears. Larry got up out of the chair and paid him.

"Muchas gracias, señor," Tony said. He had been somewhat less than garrulous while working on the Texan, and now he looked at the broken window sorrowfully, not saying anything.

Larry said: "Sorry, Tony—I almost forgot." He took

25

some folding money from his pocket and passed it over. "This cover it?"

Tony's eyes brightened. *Si, señor*—ees plenty—"

Larry cut into his voluble thanks. "Who was the hombre I had trouble with, Tony?"

"Nick?" Tony opened his hands in a gesture that seemed to say everyone knew Nick Trellis. "Nick works for Charley Allison in the Casino. He deals faro."

Larry frowned. He had sensed something behind Nick's obvious excuse for picking a quarrel. The man had come primed for trouble. Why? Larry had never run into Nick before. Evidently the gambler had been sent by someone interested in seeing that he was either scared out of Douglas or killed.

The thought annoyed the big Texan. He didn't like the way Albright had talked to him, and he resented being dragged into the trouble riding the Timberlake ranges.

He shrugged. "Well, Nick dealt himself the wrong hand this time," he said, and reached for his coat. A man came into the shop and paused just inside the door to stare at the broken window.

Tony said: "Good mornin', Meester Carsons."

The name swung Larry around, as he remembered that Carsons was the name on the envelope he had taken from Bates' body.

Carsons was a tall, spare man with the stiff bearing of a cavalry officer and the look of a Southern colonel. He said: "Mawnin', Tony. Looks like you had a bit of trouble in here."

Tony was vigorously brushing the chair seat. "*Si*, Meester Carsons—" He glanced meaningly at Brennan.

Carsons hung an expensive gray Stetson on a hook and then let his gaze rest with sharp interest on the Texan. "So yo're the gentleman who had the trouble with Nick," he said.

Larry was getting into his coat. He did not miss the thick Southern accent, nor the note of authority in the man's voice. He turned and faced him, letting his glance take in the tough leanness of this newcomer in expensive town clothes.

Carsons was in his middle fifties, and despite his grooming he looked it. He had a long bony face, arrogantly dominated by a hawk nose, and iron gray hair worn long and combed back past his ears. It matched his small waxed mustache and trim goatee. A stickpin glittered in a silk cravat.

"Trouble has a habit of gettin' around fast," Larry observed; then he nodded. "Yeah—I'm that man."

Carsons allowed the obsequious Tony to help him out of his coat before answering. "Yo' sure put yo'self in the way of trouble, suh," he said. "Nick isn't the kind of gentleman to let a thing like that go."

"Too bad for Nick," Larry said coldly.

Carsons let a thin smile come to his lips. "You have business in Douglas?"

Larry shrugged. "I don't know yet."

"Lookin' fo' work?"

Larry wondered what was behind the question. "Not particularly."

Carsons loosened his cravat. "I'm Mark Carsons," he said, and the way he said it conveyed the extent of his arrogance. He was important and powerful, he knew it, and he expected everyone else to know it. "Drop around to my office in the bank," he said casually. "I can use a man of yo' caliber."

Larry looked at him without interest. "Doin' what?"

"Yo' look like a man who can't be pushed around," Carsons replied. "We can use a man like you in the Citizens' Committee. A town organization," he explained briefly, "to see that justice is done. There's been an outbreak of killings lately, and Douglas could use a town marshal who would keep order."

"What about the sheriff's office?"

Carsons shrugged. "McVail and Albright have their hands full with the beginning of a range war. We could use a good man whose business would be to keep order in town." He paused, a sudden thought bringing a frown to his face. "Yo' one of the new Ace of Spades riders?"

"No," Larry said. "I'm just a stranger here."

Carsons seemed relieved. He walked to the chair and settled his long frame into it. "Think it over," he said.

Larry got his hat from a hook and tipped it casually over his left eye. "Mebbe I will," he replied shortly, and went out.

Chapter 5
Vanity Carsons

The drizzle had stopped. The gray cloud mass over town was breaking up under a high wind. The buildings had a raw wetness that gave a cheerless aspect to his glance.

Brennan headed for the telegraph office. He paused on

the corner of Lodestone Avenue, his glance picking up the sign midway down the block.

Then his attention was caught by the girl on the opposite corner. She was carrying a bag piled with groceries and all Larry could see of her face was a dinky straw hat perched above the groceries.

She hesitated, stepped gingerly down on the planks some-one had laid out as a crosswalk over the muddy street, and started toward him.

Larry saw the buckboard as he turned away. It was coming down Lodestone Avenue at a mad run. Some fool kid was standing up and whipping a team of grays and yelling like a wild Indian.

The girl heard the approaching buckboard and the boy's yells and stopped. The bag interfered with her vision. The kid saw her hesitate in the road and started to saw back on the reins. He managed to swerve the team slightly away from her when she unaccountably began to run.

Larry swung back and ran toward her. She was still clinging to her bag of groceries and didn't see him. She ran into him, bounced back, and sat down on the crosswalk before Larry could prevent it. Her groceries spilled into the mud.

Larry bent down and pulled her away just as the buckboard swept past. Iron tires kicked up mud that splattered Brennan and the girl. The white-faced youngster kept going down the street without looking back.

"Damn fool kid—" Larry growled, then caught himself and bent over the girl. She was sitting on the muddy boards, surprised and breathless, not yet fully comprehending what had happened. The straw hat was crushed down over a blue eye and a bunch of carrots lay like a bouquet in her lap.

"Sorry I had to be so rough," Larry said. "Let me help you up."

He held out his hands to her and when she took them he pulled her to her feet.

The girl straightened her hat, looked down at the mud on her clothes, and grimaced: "Ugh! I'm a mess. But I should be thankful it wasn't worse—"

"Too bad about yore clothes," Larry broke in. "But I didn't expect you to run and I couldn't fend you off." He smiled. "Can I see you home?"

The girl was young, not more than eighteen. She had a young girl's freshness and a woman's sadness—they were mixed up in her and the combination made her moody and shy. She was slim and small and blonde—she would have been prettier if there had been less gravity and more laughter in her eyes.

She said: "I—well—yes—thank you, mister—"

"Brennan," Larry said. "Larry Brennan."

She acknowledged the introduction with a fleeting smile that dimpled her cheeks.

"I'm Vanity Carsons," she replied. "My father is Mark Carsons."

She turned quickly as if she had said too much, and started to pick up the scattered groceries. Larry helped her, filling his pockets with cans and vegetables. They crossed to the boardwalk and Larry said: "I'm a stranger in town, Miss Carsons. You'll have to tell me where you—"

He stopped and looked past her to the riders coming down the street.

Bob Masters was astride a handsome buckskin, riding beside the buckboard driven by his sister. Even at that distance Larry could sense the violence in the slight youngster with the coldly handsome face and the yellow-flecked eyes. There was a restlessness in the kid that sought outlet even as he rode—his gaze shifted constantly from road to buildings as if expecting trouble and willing to meet it halfway.

Lennie sat stiffly, looking straight ahead. There was a proud, almost snobbish tilt to her head—and Larry felt the unyielding quality of this girl who had fashioned a shell of bitter reserve about herself. .

Her glance caught Brennan and the Carsons girl, and at the same instant Bob saw them. The youngster started to swing the buckskin away from the buckboard.

Larry felt the girl by his side tense. He glanced down at her, noticed her confusion; then his gaze went back to the hard-faced youngster. Lennie had leaned toward Bob and said something that brought him back to her side.

They rode past. Bob Masters looked back once, and Larry knew that Vanity Carsons and not he was the object of the youngster's glance. Then they turned a corner and went out of sight.

Larry looked down at Vanity. "You know the Masterses?"

"Yes," she said. Her voice was soft. In that moment he sensed desire and sadness in it. "Yes, I know them well." Then she looked up and said without emotion, "I live around the corner. Opposite the bank."

Nick Trellis sat in a chair in Charley Allison's office in the Casino. His face was swathed in bandages that left only his mouth, nose and eyes free. His right arm was in a sling. Glass had gashed it from wrist to elbow.

He sat slumped back in the chair, his eyes sullen, listening to Allison.

"Damn it, Nick," Charley said from behind his desk, "I told you not to underestimate that Texan. I had a look at him last night and I knew he would be hard to handle. Then, after Saber slipped up in the El Dorado, I figgered you'd be the man to stop him."

Trellis had a cigarette burning between the fingers of his left hand. He brought it to his lips and took a deep puff. "I'll not make that mistake next time," he said harshly. His fingers shredded the burning cigarette between them and let the pieces fall. "I can still use my left hand—"

"You'll need more than yore left hand to stop him," Allison growled. He got up and paced to the window. "We've got to stop Brennan," he snapped without looking around. He stood tall and square-shouldered against the window. "And we've got to stop that Triangle herd from being turned over to the Tumbling H."

Johnson, a lanky killer with a straw between his thin lips, said: "How much does this Texan know, Charley?"

"Too much!" Allison snapped. He turned and came back to the desk. "Brennan has the Kansas Pacific letter. Bates took it out of my desk last night while I was downstairs." He walked around the desk and sat down, scowling. "I thought the old bum was prowling around too much lately. Caught him going through my desk once before when I had him up here to clean out the place. Last night Saber followed him upstairs and caught him going through my things again. . . ."

"The old bum had more life in him than I thought," Saber said defensively. The gunman was a lean, swarthy half-breed with red hair. He was a violent-tempered man, handy with a knife and quick with a Colt. He was one of Allison's newly hired Ace of Spades hands.

"I still don't know how he got away from me in the dark, after I practically buried my knife in him. . . ."

"You don't know how Brennan got away from you either," Allison sneered. "What in hell am I paying you for, Saber—for excuses?"

The swarthy gunman scowled.

Johnson cut in quickly. "We could get Gans down from the ranch. Let him pick a fight with Brennan and—"

"No!" Allison took a cigarette from a box and lighted it. "A thing like that might get the town down on us. And the law."

"You can handle McVail," Johnson said. "And if Albright starts gettin' too big for his badge—"

Allison shook his head. "I got a better idea. Brennan

came north with that herd for Halliday. Well, Halliday's dead. Maybe if I work my cards right . . ."

He got up without finishing. "Saber," he ordered brusquely, "stay out of sight for a while. Brennan might have recognized you last night. Johnson, come with me. I want to have a talk with Brennan. . . ."

The Carsons home was a spacious house with a Georgian front and a quiet air of affluence. A white picket fence enclosed an acre of land, and trees shaded an expanse of lawn.

Vanity opened a small side gate and Larry followed her up a flagged walk to the rear of the house. The girl stopped and said: "I'll have Sue take the groceries."

She rapped on the screen door and called: "Susie!" After a while a fat negro woman appeared. She took a look at Vanity's clothes and threw her hands up in the air. ":Miss Vanity, what done happened tuh yuh?"

"Never mind the clothes," Vanity said firmly. "The mud will wash off. Here—take these groceries from this gentleman and quit your wailing."

Susie grumblingly complied. A voice from inside the house called sharply: "Vanity! Vanity Carsons! You come right inside this minute!"

Larry caught a glimpse of a small woman in black crinoline looming up behind the screen door.

He raised his hat. "Good day, Miss Carsons."

"Good day, Mister Brennan." She smiled shyly and went into the house.

Larry grinned to himself as the older woman's shocked voice came to him. "What am I going to do with you, Vanity—taking up with perfect strangers? I'll have to speak to your father."

Larry turned and went down the steps. He was coming out on the street when he noticed Mark Carsons just entering the front gate. The elder Carsons stopped, looked at Larry, then slammed the gate and walked rapidly to the front door.

Larry walked back to Lodestone Avenue and found the telegraph office.

The clerk was a natty fellow in a silk shirt and with a long waxed mustache. He took the message Larry wrote out and read it back:

"John Barstow, Triangle Ranch, Brazos County, Texas. Halliday dead. What next? Larry."

Brennan paid him. "When will he get it?"

"Tomorrow," the clerk said. "Some time tomorrow."

"I'm stayin' at the El Dorado," Larry informed him. "I'll be around in a couple of days for the answer. But if I should be out when it comes in, leave word with the hotel clerk."

"Sure, Mister Brennan," the clerk agreed. "I'll see that you get it right away."

Heels made a warning sound on the threshold. The clerk glanced up and suddenly took a step away from Larry, his eyes wary.

Charley Allison looked almost foppish in the daylight. He had on a new, tight-fitting coat that matched his expensive pearl-gray Stetson, his face was impeccably groomed, and the bulge of a shoulder holster barely showed under his right arm.

The gunman who accompanied him was a lanky man with a starboard list and a low-slung .45 on his right hip. He stepped aside as Charley paused, and stood watching Larry. He had a piece of straw between his lips and he chewed absently on the end of it.

Allison said: "I've been looking for you, Brennan."

So Allison reads registers, too, Larry thought, and shrugged. "Yo're lookin' right at me," he said casually. "What's on yore mind?"

"Cows," Charley said. "Let's go some place for a couple of drinks and talk it over."

Larry looked at the gunman lounging carelessly against the wall. "All right," he said. "Let's go talk it over."

Chapter 6
Lennie Masters Decides

Just what drove Bob Masters no one in Timberlake Valley knew.

Bob had grown up on the Tumbling H range as free and as wild as the horses he trapped in the country beyond the Diamond Heads. His mother had died shortly after coming to the Tumbling H, and Halliday, a bachelor, had never been able to cope with him.

The kid had started drifting when he was fourteen, fol-lowing the mustang herds in summer, the geese in winter. He stayed away from the Tumbling H for months at a time. Sometime during his wanderings, he learned to use a six-gun—learned to use it with deadly efficiency.

He was hotheaded and given easily to violence. When

32

trouble began to plague the Tumbling H in the form of Allison's Ace of Spades, he wanted to fight back. He got his first boost toward a killer reputation when he shot Lemery, Ace of Spades foreman, in a dispute over boundaries. Lemery had a reputation as a badman but he didn't even clear holster.

A few days later Silvers, another Ace of Spades gunman with a Tombstone reputation, passed the word around he was going to kill young Masters on sight. The kid rode into Douglas alone, sought out the killer in the Open House Saloon and taunted the suddenly nerveless gunman into drawing.

Silvers was buried the next day without honors in the growing cemetery on the hill above the trail town.

After that men began to talk softly about this wild kid whom no man could control—who heeded no one except his sister.

About Lennie Masters, tongues wagged as discreetly—and destructively. Lennie Masters usually kept to herself on the Tumbling H. She had few friends. When she came to town she carried her shell of aloofness with her—cold, proud, reserved.

"Too high an' mighty for us common folk," the tongues wagged. "And her an orphan, too. Ain't no secret that Mary Masters came to live with her brother Jeff on the Tumbling H because her husband left her to run off with another woman."

This last was pure speculation, but it made good gossip. And all the suspicions, the sneering hostility of narrow-minded townsmen was felt by the Masterses as they rode down Douglas' main street that morning and headed for Sam Luce's Funeral Parlors.

Socrates Sam met them at the door. He had been working late into the night and his eyes were tired and red-rimmed. He said: "Good morning, Lennie. Howdy, Bob."

Lennie nodded stiffly. "We've come for him."

Sam said gently: "You going to bury him on the Tumbling H?"

"Yes," Lennie's voice was strained. "Yes. Uncle Jeff wanted to be buried on his own land, and the Tumbling H is still his—at least until the end of the month."

"It'll always be his—and ours!" Bob said roughly. He had been looking down at the embalmed figure in the pine wood casket, and now he turned. He was only twenty, but he looked older. He looked like a man who had never been a boy—who had passed straight from childhood into manhood.

"Uncle Jeff settled on the upper Timberlake when Douglas was a crossroads to town. No one's goin' to take his brand away from him—alive or dead!"

Sam shrugged. "Allison's got gun backin'," he said slowly. "An' after the end of the month he'll have the law on his side."

"The law," Bob sneered, "has always been on his side. You know that as well as I do, Sam."

"You're makin' a mistake about Albright," Sam said quietly. "He don't say much, but he's honest—an' he hates Allison. About McVail—"

"Some day I'm gonna kill McVail," the kid said. He said it dispassionately. "I'm gonna kill him for what happened the night I cornered Charley Allison in the Casino, right after his men ran off the last of our stock."

"You could never prove it," Sam said. "Neither could Jeff, An' McVail only did what he had to do, because he's sheriff of this county, an' you had no proof."

"Proof!" Bob Masters' eyes flared with that yellow wildness. "I was out there that night Dan an' Reilley were killed —I saw them. But it was my word against a dozen of Allison's men—an' McVail had to stop me when I braced Charley!" He laugher bitterly. "They think they've won now —with their legal trap. Cows on the Tumblin' H ranges by October first or Carsons forecloses and the ranch goes up for auction. Damn it, Sam—they may have the law on their side, come the first of the month—but they'll have to back it with guns!"

Sam took his pipe from his mouth and stared into the street, knowing that much of what young Masters had said was true and there was little that could be done about it. Sam had been Jeff's friend for thirty years—they had come into Timberlake Valley together.

"Something may happen before the end of the month," Lennie said quietly. She was making an effort to appear unconcerned, but Sam read the helplessness in her eyes and saw behind her reserve a frightened girl who had grown up on the Tumbling H and would now be set adrift.

"Jeff told me last week he was expecting help from an old friend in Texas," he said. "Somethin' about a herd on the trail—"

Lennie nodded. "I wrote the letter for Uncle Jeff—to a man named Barstow. It was Uncle's last hope. But it looks like the herd won't get here in time—if it ever does."

Sam relighted his pipe. "If Bob wasn't so touchy," he said slowly, "you would have found out last night."

Bob turned and looked at him with hard eyes. "What are you gettin' at?"

"That big feller who slapped you around last night," Sam said. "His name's Larry Brennan. He's the man yore uncle's been expectin'. He's that trail boss from Texas."

Lennie said: "Oh!" in a small, surprised voice.

Bob frowned. "Why didn't he come out to the Tumbling H?"

"Mebbe because he had instructions to meet Jeff here," Sam said.

Lennie Masters nodded. "I remember the letter. He was to take a room at the El Dorado and wait for Uncle Jeff to contact him. We'll have to see him, Bob," she said, turning to her brother. "Tell him we're sorry about last night—"

Bob sneered, and Sam frowned, noting the wildness in the kid. "Bob," he said solemnly, "Don't make a mistake about this Texan."

"If yo're thinkin' about what happened last night, forget it," Masters said.

Sam shrugged. "I wasn't thinkin' about yore run-in with him. But a lot has happened since. If he's on yore side you can be thankful. A tougher man never came up the Texas trail."

"What happened, Sam?" Lennie asked curiously. "You sound as if you had something to tell."

"I have," Sam said. "I heard things here an' there. Asked questions. This Texan took a room in the El Dorado—the same room Jeff was killed in. Along 'bout one o'clock there was a shot. Albright happened to be in the hotel bar. He an' some of the boys went up—an' found Bates dead in Brennan's room."

"Bates!" Bob frowned. "Ain't that Allison's swamper?"

Sam nodded. "No one saw Bates go upstairs. But they found blood on the stairs and in the hall, just in front of this Texan's door, so they figger Bates was dyin' when he got there. How he got past Velie, the night clerk, without bein' seen is a question—but mebbe Velie was asleep. Anyway, this Texan acts dumb when Albright questions him. Claims he never saw Bates before in his life an' didn't know why Bates came to his room."

"Sounds like the truth," Lennie said. "It is strange that—"

"Yes, very strange," Sam said, and looked at her. "Unless Bates didn't know Jeff had been killed, which is possible, an' went to the El Dorado to see yore uncle."

"But why?" the girl said. "What could Bates have wanted with Uncle Jeff? Bates was nothing but a tramp."

"But he worked for Allison," Bob said swiftly, his eyes

searching Sam's face. "What did Albright have to say about it, Sam?"

"If Albright had anythin' to say he kept it to himself, like he always does," Sam replied. "All I know is that he brought Bates in here last night an' asked me to fix him up in a box. He'd see that Bates got buried."

Bob frowned and started to pace. Lennie said: "We saw Mister Brennan this morning. He was talking to the Carsons girl as if he had known her all his life."

Bob turned, as if the memory hurt. He said softly: "Don't say anythin' about Vanity, Lennie—not here. An' not now!"

Lennie stiffened. Sam broke in swiftly. "He gets around all right. Mornin' wasn't half begun when he had trouble with Nick Trellis, over in Tony's barbershop."

"I noticed Tony's window as we rode in," Bob said. "What happened?"

Sam chuckled. "Nick tried to shove Brennan around an' the Texan heaved him through it."

"What?"

Sam nodded. "Nick's been havin' his way around town so long he never thought it could happen to him. He's laid up now, with his gun arm in a sling. Lucky for him he didn't break his neck."

There was silence in the mortuary, until finally Lennie said: "Uncle Jeff had something on his mind these past weeks, Sam. Something he wouldn't tell even me. Do you know what it was?"

Sam shook his head. "I came into Timberlake Valley with yore uncle," he replied, and recalled that day. He had been driving a wagon down the Timber Pass trail and pulled up to watch the lean, dour man at the head of the small bunch of Texas longhorns.

"Howdy," Jeff had said. "Aimin' to settle in Douglas?"

It seemed like yesterday, but it had been all of thirty years ago.

"Good graze an' good timber," Jeff had said. "Some day my cattle will graze over half this valley. . . ." Then he had looked down from his seat astride a rangy bay and smiled with dry humor. "An' mebbe, some day, you'll be around to bury me."

All this, and the thirty years he had known Jeff Halliday, stirred in Sam at that moment. Then he shrugged and said: "No, Jeff didn't tell me anythin'. He was waitin' for that Triangle herd from Texas, that all."

"Jeff was too easygoin'," Bob said. "I told him there was only one way to fight Allison—the way he's fightin' us. It's

36

no secret the Ace of Spades has been hirin' gunslingers. But McVail won't make a move to stop Allison, an' Albright takes his orders from McVail. But I'll kill Allison first, before I let him take possession of the Tumbling H!"

"There's been enough killin'," Sam said. He turned to the coffin where Jeff's body lay, and suddenly he looked old and a little comical in his stovepipe hat and corncob pipe.

"Yo're not very popular in Douglas," he said finally, meeting Bob's eyes. "There's talk goin' around *you* killed yore uncle. The talk's been growin'. The Citizens' Committee is threatenin' action. Bob, if I were you I'd go back to the ranch an' lay low for a while until all this talk blows over."

Lennie said sharply: "You don't believe Bob killed Uncle Jeff, do you?"

"No," Sam said dryly. "But what I believe is not what the law will think, Lennie. Albright isn't sayin' anythin'—he never does. He's waitin' for McVail to get back. But there's Velie's story that he heard Bob and Jeff arguin' an'—"

"Sure," Bob broke in harshly. "We had an argument. Uncle Jeff got violent an' slapped me, an' I hit him."

He turned as Lennie made a small, startled sound. "Yes," he said savagely. "I hit him. But I didn't kill him. Lennie, you know we never got along. An' last night he said somethin' I couldn't take—"

"The Carsons girl?"

"Yes!" Bob snapped, white-lipped. "Vanity Carsons!"

Lennie's lips pursed. "After what her father called you! After he warned you, publicly, to stay away from her—"

Sam placed a hand on her arm and shook his head. "This is not the place for a family quarrel. I should think you'd have some respect for the dead."

Lennie relaxed. "All right, Sam. It's not pretty, fighting over Jeff's body. Will you give us a hand with the coffin? We'll take him with us now."

Sam nodded. "I'll be out to the ranch tomorrow," he said. "Unless you'd rather be alone?"

"You know we'd like to have you," Lennie told him.

The coffin was not heavy, and between them Bob and Sam carried it out to the buckboard. Sam paused. "If this Texan has the cattle Jeff was waitin' for he came just in time," he suggested.

Bob glanced down the street. "You say he's stayin' at the El Dorado?"

Sam nodded. "Don't forget what I said, Bob. He's not one to be pushed—"

"I'll be nice to him!" Bob sneered. "I'll treat him with kid gloves!"

Lennie was getting into the buckboard, but she stopped as if Bob's tone had crystallized some decision. She came back and held Bob's arm as he prepared to mount the buckskin.

"I'll see Brennan," she said. Her voice was quietly determined. "You take the buckboard back to the ranch." She brushed aside Bob's protests. "We've had enough trouble," she went on. "I'll handle this my way."

She waited until Bob climbed angrily into the buckboard and drove away. Then she mounted Bob's horse. "We'll be expecting you tomorrow, Sam," she said.

Sam watched her ride down the street, stiff and erect—and after a while he shook his head and went back inside.

Chapter 7

Open Break

Larry Brennan followed Allison and his gun hireling, Johnson, to the Casino, a false-fronted building at the corner of Main and Texas Avenue.

The big gambling hall was deserted at that early morning hour . . . faro and monte tables were covered . . . the roulette wheels stilled. A half-dozen hard-eyed customers lounged against the long bar, listening idly to a small, silk-shirted individual with gaudy arm bands playing melodies on the piano.

Wide stairs curved up to an open balcony. Nick Trellis was coming down these stairs. He saw Larry and stopped. He watched Larry cross the room to the bar with Allison and Johnson. Then he turned and went back upstairs.

Larry noticed the gambler and wariness came to the Texan. He loosened his coat and kept his eye on the open balcony as he walked to the bar. The bartender, a rawboned man with drooping handlebar mustache, scurried over.

"Get me a bottle of Old Taylor," Allison said. "And three glasses."

The bartender brought the bottle and the glasses and Allison took them and turned toward a table. "Let's sit, Brennan," he said pleasantly. "It's friendlier."

Larry shrugged. He took a seat so that he faced the balcony. Johnson pulled out a chair, reversed it, and sat down, resting his long arms across the top. He faced Larry across the table, his eyes blank and unsmiling.

Allison filled the glasses. "Nothing like having a drink

from private stock," he said conversationally. "I own the Casino and I always make sure my friends get the best."

Larry leaned back in his chair. "You didn't bring me here to drink good whiskey," he said. "What's on yore mind?"

Allison smiled. "Cows." He took a cigar from his vest pocket, held it out to the Texan. Larry shook his head. Allison shrugged, unhurriedly cut off one end of the smoke with a small pocket knife, and lighted it.

"You brought a herd up the trail," he opened. "I want to buy it."

"It ain't for sale," Larry said.

"I'll give you a good price. More'n you can get anywhere in the section."

"They're still not for sale."

Allison frowned. The gunman at his side chewed slowly, his eyes on Larry. The piano tinkled softly in the big room.

"Look!" the Ace of Spades rancher said bluntly. "I'm going to lay my cards face up on the table. I know you came up the trail with cows for Halliday. Well, Halliday's dead. That leaves you with a herd on your hands. I'm willing to pay you five dollars a head over and above the market price. In cash. And I'll take your tally."

Larry took his time answering. He was wondering how much these Triangle cows meant in this game being played for control of the Timberlake ranges. Halliday had indicated in his letter he needed the cattle or he'd go broke. And now the boss of the Ace of Spades was making his bid. Larry had to admit it was a pretty strong bid.

"They're not mine to sell," he finally answered. "I just work for the Triangle; I don't own it."

"You're the trail boss," Allison persisted. "You came up here and found the man you were to deliver the herd to dead. A thousand miles. Why sweat out another thousand trailing them back? It's not good business."

"No," Larry agreed. "It's not good business. But I had orders to turn those cows over to Halliday, an' until I get different orders they stay where they are."

Anger reddened Allison's face—the anger of a man not used to being balked.

"You're a hard man to do business with, Brennan," he snapped, losing his temper. "Don't forget—there're other ways. A stampede some dark night"—he looked across at Brennan, his eyes hard and unfriendly now—"and the cows you sweated to bring out here will be scattered over half of Colorado!"

Larry stiffened. "Thanks for tellin' me."

"You still refuse?"

"I said that beef wasn't mine to sell!" the Texan said angrily. Damn it, he hadn't asked for chips in this game. He had come on a purely routine job to deliver a bunch of cows to a man named Halliday. But he had a stubborn streak and Allison's threats rubbed him the wrong way.

"You wanted to talk business—you got my answer!" He tossed a coin on the table and started to get up. "That's for the drink," he said contemptuously. "I only let my friends treat."

The lanky gunman with the poker face said: "You gonna let this—get away with it, Charley?"

Larry lunged across the table and got a fistful of the gunman's vest and shirt and jerked him halfway across the table.

"All right," he sneered. "You been sittin' here, lookin' tough an' sayin' nothin'. *What are you goin' to do about it?*"

Johnson jerked loose and started to rise. Larry cuffed him to the floor. And in that same moment Nick Trellis appeared on the balcony—a gun in his left hand.

His first shot splintered into the table in front of Brennan; his second went up into the ceiling as the Texan's shot tore into him. He took a step forward, fell against the railing, and toppled over. He landed with a sudden thud on top of the piano.

The piano player fell backward off his stool when Nick hit the piano . . . his last chords fading into the jarring discord caused by Nick's fall.

Larry stood crouched, a wisp of smoke curling up from his long-barreled Colt. The lanky gunman was on the floor, not moving. Allison was stiff in his chair, his hands in plain sight, his lips tight around his cigar.

The Texan's cold eyes ranged to the men standing rigid at the bar and the threat in his eyes held them motionless. His glance came back to Allison.

"I don't like bein' strong-armed into business deals!" he said flatly. "An' I don't like bein' set up as a target. Next time you hire a man to do a job see that you get one who can shoot straight."

Allison wet his lips.

"You got anythin' more to say?" Larry snapped.

"No!" The Ace of Spades boss' voice was soft—and dangerous. "Nothing more to say."

"Then I'll speak my piece," Larry said tightly. "If somethin' happens to that Triangle herd someone's gonna get hurt. Remember that, Allison. If you want trouble, try runnin' off those cows. There's a bunch of Texans who'll see that you get it—even if we have to ride out to yore ranch to bring it to you!"

"That's big talk," Allison smiled faintly. "I'll remember it."

Larry sneered. His glance flicked out to the men at the bar, then came back to the white-faced gunman who had not moved from where he had been cuffed to the floor.

"You've got a big mouth—when you open it," he said softly. "I'm gonna give you yore chance to back yore talk."

The Texan holstered his Colt and stood there, waiting. And then, when no one moved, he backed slowly to the doors, turned, and went out.

Strain lingered in the room, dissipating slowly, like fine mist under a burning sun.

Charley Allison stared toward the slatted doors, his eyes ugly with unmasked feeling. The piano player got up, looked at Nick's sprawled body, and walked white-faced and shaken to the bar.

"Give me a drink, Barney—quick!" he said, and his voice broke the curious stillness with its discordancy.

The men at the bar relaxed and turned back to their drinks. Johnson got to his feet. Methodically he began to pull his shirt down under his belt.

"I'm goin' to kill him for that, Charley," he said.

Allison looked up at him. "Not in an even break," he retorted. "You saw what happened to Nick." His lips flattened around his cigar. "I didn't know Nick was gonna be that much of a fool. You saw it. That Texan's too good for you, Ira—in an even break!"

Ira Johnson reached for the bottle of Old Taylor and poured himself a drink. His hand shook. "I'm not a fool," he said harshly. He was burning with such suppressed rage that it caused a nerve to jump in his cheek. "But he's not goin' to get away with it, Charley. No man can slap me around like that an' get away with it!"

Allison chewed on his cigar. "Maybe you'll have your chance—the way you want it" His eyes were narrow and calculating as he looked at Johnson.

"I got a hunch that Brennan's going out to that Triangle herd this morning. You heard what he wired his boss. He'll have to hang around for a few days doing nothing, and it's a good bet now that he'll ride out to tell his men what happened. You know this country better than most of us, Ira. Follow him. Find out where he's keeping that herd. What you do afterward is up to you. But find out where that herd is first!"

41

Johnson nodded. He poured himself a drink with steadier hand. Color was coming back into his long hard face.

"I'll be waiting at the ranch," Allison said. His eyes were flat and ugly with emotion. "By hell, Brennan asked for it—and he's going to get it! We'll run those cows off if we have to kill every Texan guarding them—and if Brennan's alive when it's over, I'll be waiting for him!"

Johnson nodded. "I'll borrer Nig," he said tonelessly. "That big black of yourn kin cover a lot of territory."

Allison nodded. "Remember," he warned, "find out where they're keeping that Triangle herd first, before you try to get even with Brennan. We've had two slip-ups already. Don't make a third."

"I won't!" Johnson said coldly.

Allison watched the lanky gunman go out. Then he got up and walked to Nick's body. He stared down at the swarthy gambler. Nick had bungled his chance at the Texan, but maybe he could make something out of it.

He walked back to the bar. Five of the men at the rail he knew well—they'd say what he told them to. The sixth—his eyes fastened on the back of the man's sunburned neck. He was a surly nester from Grizzly Hollow, and could be persuaded to keep silent.

"Barney!" he called the bartender. "Go out and get the law. Tell Albright Brennan just killed Nick—without giving Nick a chance to draw his gun."

Barney stared.

"Go on!" Allison snapped. "Get him!"

The bartender gulped. "Sure, Charley—sure. I'll get him."

Allison walked to the dead man again, and found his Colt. He slipped in two cartridges, replacing those Nick had fired. Then he placed the Colt back in Nick's clip holster.

Walking to the bar, he went around the counter and faced the men leaning on the rail. "What are you boys having? It's on the house."

Albright was in the sheriff's office, his booted feet crossed on the desk, taking things easy and wishing McVail would get back. Things were beginning to pop in town, and so far he had gotten nowhere on who had killed Halliday and Bates.

He wasn't entirely sold on Bob Masters as his uncle's killer, although he admitted there was no telling what that wild kid would do. But Halliday's death was too pat—and Albright wondered what McVail would do when he got back.

He shifted his cigar stub to the other side of his mouth

and was reaching in his pocket for a match when Barney popped in.

Allison's bartender opened without preamble. "That Texan, Brennan, just shot Nick Trellis. Charley wants you to come over and see."

Albright scowled. He pulled his long feet off the desk and swung around. "What was Brennan doin' in the Casino, Barney?"

Barney looked flustered, "I donno," he said, and wet his lips. "Charley says for you to come over."

Albright got up and got his hat. He was a loose-limbed man with an indolent walk and Barney had to curb his pace. The bartender pushed through the Casino's doors and scurried toward the bar, leaving Albright just inside the gambling hall.

Albright didn't like Allison. It had started in a small way, right after the hard, handsome gambler came to Douglas. There had been trouble in the Casino one night and Albright had questioned Allison.

The gambler's curt replies irritated him and Allison's parting shot had never been forgotten. "Some men get too big for their badges, Albright. Don't let it happen to you!"

He looked down the length of the bar now, his gaze lingering on the half-dozen men elbowing the counter. Charley was behind the bar, smoking a fat cigar. He waited, letting Albright take in the scene; then, when the deputy began to talk toward Nick's body, he said: "What are you going to do about it, Albright?" There was a challenging sneer in his voice.

Albright made no comment. He walked to Nick, looked down at the body, then raised his eyes to the balcony above. Bending, he turned Nick over and pulled out Nick's Colt. He looked at the chamber, sniffed at the muzzle. He replaced the weapon and walked back among the tables until he found the bullet-scarred one where Brennan had been sitting.

He fingered the freshly splintered hole, glanced back at the balcony, then turned and looked at Allison.

"Next time you try to rig a frame on a man, make a good job of it, Allison. Clean his Colt an' get rid of all contrary evidence."

"There's six men here who saw it!" Allison snapped.

"Saw what?" Albright asked. His voice was flat. "Saw what you wanted them to see?"

Allison sneered. "All right, Albright. I told you once you were getting too big for that badge. We'll see how long you keep it."

43

Albright walked up to the bar, slow and indolent—and deadly. He put his hands on the counter and looked at Allison, his enmity unmasked. "The day I lose this star, Allison, I'm gonna come lookin' for yuh. Just remember that when you go about takin' it from me."

Allison laughed, but it was a short, forced laugh. The deputy turned, glanced coldly at the silent men among the rail, and walked out.

Chapter 8
Going Someplace?

Brennan left the Casino and walked swiftly back to El Dorado, where he found the day clerk filing mail in pigeon-holes behind the desk.

"I'm leavin' town for a day or two," he said. "If the law comes lookin' for me, tell him I'll be back. If a telegram comes in, file it for me."

He turned and went out, walking with long strides toward the livery stable. The sun was warm in the streets of Douglas, baking the mud, hardening the ruts in the road. He was not interrupted, and five minutes later he rode out of the Timberlake stables.

He left Douglas the way he had entered it. Once out of town, he swung west along the river trail. A half-hour later he forded the wide, shallow Timberlake River at Pebbly Crossing and turned the roan south toward higher ground.

The wind had shredded the clouds and sunlight patched the valley. There was a clean freshness in the air, as if yesterday's rain had washed it of dust and dirt.

Timberlake Valley at that point was a vast trough, its wooded slopes more than ten miles apart. The foothills in the north went mounting up to the high, rocky peaks of the San Miguels. To the south the timber and grassy meadows gave way to wilder country that gullied down to the Mesa Seco badlands.

Larry rode south along an old wagon road; when it turned off and went east he left it and kept going south. He rode by landmark now, keeping the crest of a bald knob to his left front.

He let the roan jog along, sitting easily between rim and horn, letting his thoughts run through him. There was going to be trouble and Duke and the boys would have to be warned. Allison's threat had been no idle remark. The flashily dressed rancher had something big at stake, and a handful of Texans a thousand miles from home would not stop him.

He was an hour out of Douglas when he saw the rider. He had been forced into a cutback by a wall of rock and his idle glance picked up the speck crossing a clearing between timber.

His intuition warned him. Allison was losing no time, he thought grimly, and a hard smile touched the corner of his mouth.

He let the roan take its own pace, the way it had since leaving Douglas. Fifteen minutes later he rode down into a wide gully the further bank of which was fringed with brush and small timber. A rider intent on haste might be fooled into thinking he had pushed on across the gully, his passage screened by the brush.

He dismounted and led the roan toward a shielding mesquite tree on the near bank, and tied the animal there. The bank was higher than he as he stood erect and it would hide them both effectively from anyone riding his trail.

Squatting on his heels, he slid his Colt into his hand and waited.

The sun beat down into the gully. Wind made a soft, caressing sound in the brush. A lizard came out of a hole in the embankment, slithered a few feet across the pale sand and paused to eye the motionless Texan with beady gaze.

A sound disturbed it. It darted back, paused to look at Larry, then whisked into a hole.

The sound of a running horse came plainly now. There was no caution in the sound—only haste. It drew nearer, then slowed as it neared the gully. A rider loomed up on the bank. The buckskin minced a moment on the edge, then sat back on its haunches and slid down.

Larry came forward swiftly, the Colt in his hand glinting in the sunlight. "Goin' some place?" he asked roughly.

The buckskin reared skittishly at his sudden approach. The rider, caught by surprise, was twisted out of the saddle.

Larry holstered his gun and took a swift step forward. A cream sombrero had slipped from jet black hair and lay beside the crumpled figure.

It was Lennie Masters!

He bent and slid an arm under her, raising her head and shoulders from the sand. The fall had stunned her. He brushed back hair from her face, and touched the bruise near her temple.

She was soft in his arms. Her cold reserve was gone and

45

she looked appealingly small and girlish now. He remembered the way she had looked last night, her lips curled unpleasantly. . . . They were full and soft now, and he had the sudden unfounded thought she had never been kissed.

He eased her down then and went back to his cayuse. The canteen slung from his saddle was full. He brought it back and knelt beside her. Her eyes flickered as he raised her up again.

"Here," he said. "Drink some of this."

He put the canteen to her lips and she gulped, then turned her head away. He let a few drops fall on the soft curve of her throat.

Her eyes, clouded and uncertain, searched his face.

He said: "I'm sorry I frightened you. I expected someone else."

He felt her body stiffen against his arm. She pulled away from him and sat up. He felt her hostility and a spasm of anger went through him. Bending, he lifted her roughly to her feet. He had no interest in her, nor in her troubles.

"That wasn't a smart thing to do, Miss Masters," he said coldly. "I might have shot first an' asked questions afterwards."

The girl's face was close to him and his hands were tight on her arms. He saw the hardness melt from her, as if his tone, his strength, ripped the shell of self-containment from her—for a moment there was something soft and appealing about her. Then she pulled away from him and her cold reserve was between them again, an unscalable wall.

"I tried to get you at the El Dorado," she explained brusquely. "I wanted to apologize for what happened last night."

There was little apology in her tone and Larry shrugged. He turned and walked to the buckskin who had sought the company of the Texan's roan. Larry caught the trailing reins and led the animal back to the girl.

"We were all pretty touchy last night," he said. "Let's forget it."

Lennie Masters ran probing fingers over the bruise on her face. She made a little grimace and dropped her fingers. Her hair was loose and naturally wavy; it fell like a black cloud on her shoulders.

"Sam told us who you were," she said. "That's why I followed you. I want those cattle you trailed here from Texas. The cows you were to deliver to my uncle, Jeff Halliday."

Larry shook his head. Her brusque, confident tone irritated him. "You made a mistake," he said levelly.

The girl frowned. "You *are* the Texan my uncle was ex-

46

pecting? You did come into Timberlake Valley with a herd?"

Larry nodded.

The girl stiffened. "When can you run them onto Tumbling H grass?" she demanded coldly.

"When I get an answer from my boss," Larry replied. His tone was short. "My instructions were to deliver to Halliday. There's over five hundred head involved—"

"But we're Halliday's legal heirs!" the girl interrupted. "I wrote that letter for my uncle to Barstow, and we got his wire telling us you were on the way. My uncle was killed before you arrived, but that doesn't change the picture here —nor the need for those cows, Mister Brennan. Without those cattle we lose the Tumbling H."

Larry was unmoved. "That's not my problem," he said. "If Barstow wants you to have the cattle, he'll tell me. You'll get them then."

The girl looked at him with sudden contempt. "I guess Sam was wrong about you."

"I don't know what Sam told you," Larry said dryly. "But I can't turn over those cows to you until I get an answer from Barstow."

Color came into her face, breaking the immobility of her features. "You're the stubbornest man I've ever met—if stubbornness it is that explains your action."

He reached out, picked her up off her feet and placed her in the buckskin's saddle. His motion had been swift and unexpected and left her speechless.

He stepped back and looked up at her, a smile touching his lips. "For a woman yo're too bossy. You been givin' too many orders—and sometimes, for a woman, that's bad."

"Not half as bad," she said angrily, "as a man who can't see anything but his own way!" She took the reins in her hands and looked down at him, her eyes dark and full of emotion. "The Tumbling H hasn't much left—except land. We've been rustled blind. Some of our best men have been shot. The riders we have left are not gunfighters. But we're going to fight. We're going to fight for every inch of the Tumbling H—for every blade of grass—every shack. . . ."

"You'll get the herd," Larry interrupted dryly, "when Barstow says so."

The girl's hands tightened on the reins. "We'll get those cows, Brennan," she said passionately, "even if we have to come for them! Remember that—even if we have to come for them!"

The buckskin whirled on its hind legs and scrambled back up the bank. Larry waited, listening to the drumbeat

47

of the animal's hoofs fade into the warm stillness. Then he walked to the roan and mounted.

This was the second threat against the herd he had received that morning and stubbornness rode hard in him. That Triangle herd seemed to have become the focus of the range trouble in Timberlake, and until he got Barstow's wire he and the boys would do well to be on their toes.

Chapter 9

Texans Prepare For Trouble

It was well along in the afternoon when Brennan pulled up at the entrance of a canyon whose crumbly slopes were brush-grown and baking in the sun. He had long since left the watered, timbered valley to the north ... southward the earth sloped down into the Mesa Seco sinks, a barren wasteland of scar buttes blue-hazed and remote against the horizon.

Larry looked expectantly along the frowning cliff wall and felt a stab of annoyance when he saw no one. Duke and the boys were not expecting trouble, but it would have been a wise move to have posted a man on the cliffs overlooking the canyon mouth.

He skirted the north shoulder, noting that the recent rain had been brief there, for it had not erased the tracks of the Triangle herd. His glance followed the tracks into the wasteland. He had come in from the southwest, following Halliday's instructions. The herd had swung off the Platte River trail seventy miles south of Douglas and made a wide arc through the Mesa Seco badlands to reach this canyon Halliday had marked with an X on his map.

The Tumbling H owner had wanted secrecy, and Larry now knew why he had been so cautious. Despite these precautions Allison had known he had come up the trail with Texas cattle, and from now on vigilance would be the watchword.

The roan pricked its ears as it jogged into the canyon, sensing water and companionship were ahead. Halliday had called this long, crooked slash into the red mesalong "Lost Springs Canyon." Larry had explored it curiously after the Triangle herd had been bedded down.

The canyon reached like a twisted, four-fingered hand into the rocky mesa that towered up behind it, the main, high-walled cut petering up and out into the dry, rocky heights. Three others branched off, narrowing into little more than fissures in the red, steep cliffs.

The canyon bellied out just past the narrow-mouthed entrance. The springs were there, flowing abruptly from the base of the west wall, watering a small oasis before seeping into the rocky earth. There was water and feed enough for a few days more—beyond that the Triangle herd would have to go on short rations.

Six men were lolling about a small fire and a chuck wagon when Larry rode up. The Triangle herd was grazing contentedly along the eastern wall. Two riders rode leisurely among them. Hank Sommers, the cook, was in the chuck wagon.

Duke Sayer got to his feet and followed Larry to the chuck wagon. Larry dismounted and started to strip saddle and gear from the roan, and Duke grinned: "We've been waiting for you since sunup. How did you like the sinful town of Douglas, Larry?"

Duke was tall and slight and long-legged. He was nearing thirty, but he looked like a youngster of twenty, with boyish features and brown, wavy hair. He had come to the Tumbling H green—an awkward Easterner with a Harvard accent, a habit of meticulous grooming, and an eagerness to learn. Three years later he was Brennan's right-hand man on the trail—a quick thinker and a man who could ride with the best of them.

Larry pulled his gear from the roan's back and slapped the animal on the rump. The roan tossed its head, gave a pleased whinny, and went galloping to join the remuda grazing past the far spring.

"Not as bad as Abilene," Larry said, "an' bigger'n Willow Junction." He reached into his saddle bags and drew out a couple of quarts of whiskey. "Pass 'em along—wait!" He held onto a quart. "I'd better turn one quart over to Hank —for safekeepin'."

Duke grinned. "You know what Hank will do with it. He'll drink it, then swear he used it in his baking."

"Keep an eye on him then." Larry said. He fished in his coat pocket and drew out a half-dozen cigars. "Here's a couple of them English cigars to keep yuh happy," he added.

"Thanks, Larry." Duke took the cigars; then his eyes went serious. "What's happened? Something gone wrong?"

Larry shrugged. The others were coming up. Hank came out of the chuck wagon, wiping his hands on a greasy apron. "If I git my hands on the night-prowlin' galoot who

49

swiped the last of my applejack I'll—Howdy, Larry. When do we git to town? I'm runnin' out of grub feedin' this bunch of no good, belly-robbin'—"

"Sure," Duke broke in eagerly. "We're getting quite tired of laying around, Larry. When do we break camp?"

"I don't know," Larry said. Then, as Duke frowned, he added: "Halliday's dead!"

The others came crowding around. Larry watched them, weighing them against the trouble that was coming. They were a diverse group, but they had been hand picked. He had known them all for more than two years—good men on the trail and good men in a scrap.

There was Beefy Burns who had been riding for the Triangle for more than ten years. Beefy was five feet four in his runover boots and almost as wide. Like a lot of heavy men, he was surprisingly agile, tireless on the trail, a good drag man and none better in a fight.

Chuck Wallis, tawny-haired and blue-eyed, was about Larry's age. He was slim to the point of fragility, which was an illusion. He was tougher than most men, talked little, worked hard. He wasn't good with a six-gun, but he could usually hit a running target at three hundred yards with the Winchester he kept oiled and dust-protected in his saddle boot.

Red Marder was older than any of them except Hank—a quiet, rangy man who had been with the Triangle as long as Beefy. He had been married once, but lost his wife and only child when his wagon tipped over while crossing the San Saba in flood.

Carp was a small, wiry man with a mouth like the fish he had been named after. He was a cold-blooded, reserved man in his thirties—but he wore his six-gun thonged low on his left hip. And though he was a southpaw, Larry had seen few men get a shooting iron out quicker.

Duke was dressed like a dude, which had earned him his nickname. Even on the trail he kept shaved and groomed. He was the only man who brushed his teeth regularly. He was restless, gay, intelligent—there wasn't a better man working for John Barstow.

Larry's eyes rested briefly on the last man to join the group.

"Parson" Johnny was eighteen now—he had come to the Triangle four years back, riding chuckline. Wing Lee, the Chinese cook, had given him some grub and Barstow had come upon him wolfing the food down. Barstow had taken a liking to the kid and given him a job, helping Lee at first, and later helping Jim Evers, horse wrangler.

Johnny was a slim, freckled-faced kid who kept in the

background, worked hard, never complained. The others kidded him in the rough manner of the range, told him tall tales. He listened gravely, took the joking without rancor. But Larry had come upon him several times while the others were bedded down around the campfire—caught him staring toward the dark horizon, a lonely, friendless kid.

Just how "Parson" Johnny would react to trouble was yet to be seen.

Duke broke into his train of thought. "Where does that leave us, Larry?"

Brennan said: "Holdin' a mess of trouble." He walked to the fire and hunkered down. The others gathered around and watched him pour himself a cup of coffee. They looked expectant and eager—they were tired of inactivity and they were ready to welcome trouble.

Quietly, between sips of coffee, Larry explained what had happened to him in Douglas. "I wired Barstow for instructions," he finished. "In the meantime we sit tight. If Allison comes lookin' for trouble, we'll give it to him."

Duke lit a cigarette. "Charley Allison?" He looked at Larry, his thoughts turned inward, a frown shading his face. "Dresses like a fop, talks softly, like a woman—has long fingers—gun on left hip, gun in shoulder holster under left arm. Gray eyes that are as opaque as rocks—"

Larry nodded. "Where'd you meet him, Duke?"

Duke shrugged and ground out his cigarette. "Long time ago—in St. Louis. I was on a spree, with a pocketful of money. I lost it to a man named 'Silk' Allison in the Preston House."

Larry got up. "We'll keep out of trouble—if we can. But the days of loafin' around here are over. We're gonna keep a two-man watch on the cliffs by the canyon mouth, an' a night guard around the herd. Allison's men'll know they've run into somethin' if they try to stampede this herd."

Beefy grinned. "Sounds like old times on the Triangle, Larry. Reminds me of the time the J Circle Dot tried to push through Kiowa Pass an' block us from Clear Springs. The old man rode with us that night."

He was squatting on his heels, drawing tight the drawstrings of a Bull Durham sack. He got up now, pocketing the tobacco with one hand rolling the cigarette deftly between the fingers of the other.

"Guess I'll ride out to the herd an' send Jim and Steve in," he said.

Hank wiped his hands in his apron, an unconscious ges-

51

ture with him. "I'll fix yuh up some grub, Larry. Got some beans an' a side of beef." He turned toward the chuck wagon and caught the sight of Johnny, hunkering beyond the fire. "Thought I told yuh to rustle in some firewood," he growled. "Git goin' afore it gits dark."

Larry watched the kid disappear. The others drifted off. Duke handed him a cigarette and held a light for him. Larry took a deep puff and Duke said: "What's on your mind, Larry?"

The Triangle trail boss took the letter from his pocket and handed it to the puncher with the Harvard accent. "Bates was killed because of that," he said without comment.

Duke's eyes flicked over the concise message. "So the Kansas Pacific is building through Timberlake?" He looked up at Larry. "Depends where the KP drives its survey stakes. This doesn't say. But whoever owns land the KP will build over stands to make money. A lot of it."

Larry frowned. "Halliday must have got wind of the deal," he said. "Bates came to El Dorado to sell this letter to him."

"Who was Bates?"

"Seems like he was an old bum Allison hired to clean up in the Casino."

Duke took a deep puff on his cigarette. "This letter is addressed to Carsons. You say he owns the bank in Douglas? How did Bates, a hanger-on in the Casino, get hold of it?"

"I don't know," Larry said. "Unless Allison had it in the Casino."

Duke took the cigarette out of his mouth, looked at it thoughtfully before flicking it into the fire. "That seems to tie this banker Carsons with Allison," he said. Larry said nothing, and Duke added: "Who is he?"

Larry shrugged. "Looks like a Southern colonel, talks as if he owns Douglas, an' heads a Citizens' Committee which wants to clean up the town. He offered me the job of town marshal."

Duke's eyes lightened. "You sure got around in Douglas."

Larry made no comment. He was silent and preoccupied, and after a while Duke said: "Think the old man will call us back?"

"I don't know." Larry took a last drag on his cigarette, his eyes on the two riders jogging toward the chuck wagon. He was thinking of Lennie Masters at that moment and the thought inspired his answer. "I hope not, Duke. I'd like to see this thing through."

52

Chapter 10
Death Strikes On The Timberlake

At the moment Larry was talking to Duke, a man was picking his way up the crumbly south wall of the canyon. He carried a Henry 30.40 rifle in his left hand and a pair of old Army field glasses hung from a leather thong around his sunburned neck.

Ira Johnson knew the Mesa Seco country well. He had been born and brought up in Cristobal, on the other side of the Diamond Heads. As a young man he had served as a government scout, working out of Fort Scott. He killed a man in Cristobal later, in an argument over a dancing girl, and he started to go bad after that. He drifted south to the border, got into several shady deals with border-hoppers and earned a reputation as a gunman. He drifted to St. Louis when the Rangers started making it hot for border-jumpers and it was there that he ran into Allison.

Allison had been making a living working the river boats. He got into an argument with a kid in a card game, killed him, and found he came from a Southern family with a string of quick-trigger, revenge-hunting kin-folk.

So when Allison headed west to Douglas and bought the Casino, Johnson was with him. . . . He was with the hard-eyed gambler the night Allison took along half a dozen men and forced the Terry brothers to sell the Ace of Spades.

Johnson had been in from the beginning and he felt he had a stake in the outcome of the squeeze-play that was forcing the Tumbling H into bankruptcy and making the Ace of Spades the most profitable venture with which he had ever been connected.

Following Brennan had not been hard. Because he knew the country and could read tracks like a Ute, he let the big Texan leave town and get well out of sight before saddling Allison's big black and taking up the trail.

He caught sight of Lennie Masters before she saw him and pulled off the trail to let her pass. Then he followed her and watched the meeting with Brennan. He could have killed Brennan then, but he agreed with Allison that the herd came first. There would be time later. . . .

Johnson had the Indian's instinct for land and direction, and after Brennan parted from the Masters girl and headed south Johnson made a shrewd guess concerning direction and general destination. To save time and keep out of sight, just in case Brennan got suspicious and came back, he cut across country. Several times he stopped to pick up the Texan with his glasses, and the last ten miles he had paralleled Brennan down into the Mesa Seco country.

He left the black well hidden and after a careful survey he climbed the canyon wall. He pulled himself over the top and lay flat, his sharp eyes picking up and holding every bit of cover that might conceal an armed guard. Seeing no one, he smiled, his blue eyes a little contemptuous. They were either careless, or very sure of themselves, these Texans. They had not even placed a lookout on the canyon walls.

The sun was slipping down onto the shoulders of the western hills. Daylight was fading fast in the canyon and Johnson had a lot of checking to do before it grew too dark to see.

Running like a crouched Apache, the rifle held close in at his waist, he crossed the space to the canyon rim. He went down to his hands and knees and squirmed the last few feet on his stomach.

The sun slanted across his lanky frame. Johnson kept his Henry behind him, careful lest some reflection from its barrel betray him to the men below.

Shading his glasses from the sun, he studied the scene in the canyon for long, patient minutes. His mind made notes of the number of cows, the men sprawled around the chuck wagon, the rider on the edges of the herd. He checked and rechecked every man.

He counted ten men, including Larry and the cook.

Johnson laughed at the grim irony of things. It was a strange twist of Fate that had made the Texans pick the only spot in which to hold the Triangle herd that would give the Ace of Spades all the advantage.

Fooled by what was apparently a box canyon with no outlet save the desert entrance, the Triangle men would be on guard against trouble only from the north.

But Johnson was one of the few men who knew the secret of Lost Springs Canyon. He had trailed a band of Utes through there years before, when he was a government scout. The Utes had stolen a bunch of government horses and used the canyon to shake off their pursuers.

There was a crack in the west wall of one of the angling fingers of the canyon, heavily screened with boxwood and cottonwoods. The crack became a path that tunneled into the wall ... it opened onto the darkness of a cave under the mesa. The way was a damp and treacherous one over wet rock, and off in the darkness a stream fretted against the dark walls, losing itself underground before emerging from the cave.

The Utes had come that way with the stolen horses, negotiating the treacherous passage that finally opened to a small, well watered valley in the hills beyond the mesa.

Those Triangle men would never know what hit them when Ace of Spades riders came through that passageway into the canyon.

The thin smile remained on Johnson's face as he crawled back and made his way down the crumbly wall. He mounted and rode north, keeping away from the canyon entrance and not crossing Brennan's tracks.

A mile from the canyon he found his campsite... a shallow wash that held a fringe of brush and some spiky grass. The black could forage there and be hidden from anyone climbing the canyon cliffs. The country between him and the canyon was fairly level and from the rise behind him he could survey the entrance with his glasses.

He went back, watered the black, staked it down the wash. He took no chances on a fire. He ate a cold supper of canned beans and after dark he sat smoking, planning his next moves.

There was little danger Brennan would leave at night. The Triangle trail boss would probably leave in the morning, if he left at all.

Johnson hoped he would. The night deepened and memory of the way Brennan had humiliated him ate like acid into his thoughts.

Finally he turned in, rolling up like a cocoon in his blankets. In the distance a coyote howled mournfully as a crescent moon crept up into the star-hung sky.

Morning came with desert suddenness, cold and clear-skied. He rolled out of his blankets, ate a hasty breakfast of canned peaches, and was on the rise, scanning the canyon entrance through his glasses before the sun came up.

The sun climbed up over the Diamond Heads, spearing yellow light over the sand flats. Heat began to shimmer in the bottoms; it burned the back of Johnson's neck.

Johnson waited with the grim patience of a man who has a rendezvous with death. A man loomed up briefly on the canyon rim and disappeared, and Johnson sneered. They were finally getting cautious and setting a lookout on the cliff. A little late, he thought, and his sneer widened as he envisioned the surprise of those Triangle men when the Ace of Spades raiders hit them. . . .

A rider showed up in the canyon mouth, waved to the guard on the cliff, and headed northeast. Johnson's glasses brought Larry into closeup, and a satisfied look came into his eyes.

He watched the Texan for about five minutes, noting his direction, calculating his destination by visualizing the lay of the land ahead of Brennan. Then he slipped back, broke camp, untied the black and saddled.

If things worked out right he'd have good news to report to Allison. . . .

"I'll be back as soon as I get the old man's wire," Larry said to Duke just before he left. "Sit tight here an' be ready for trouble. If somethin' happens, send a man to Douglas for me. I'll be stayin' at the El Dorado."

Duke nodded. "Chuck's taking the first watch on the cliff," he said. "Rest of the boys are getting their guns oiled. It might be a false alarm, but it gives us something to do while waiting. Be seeing you, Larry."

"Hope it's soon," Larry said, and jogged out of the canyon. He turned to wave at Chuck, then touched heels to the roan's flanks and sent it loping north.

He had studied Halliday's rough map of the country and gained an idea of where the Tumbling H was located. He did not ride back the way he had come, but cut across a tongue of the sinks, heading for a line of ragged hills that made a blue-hazed barrier against the badlands.

He was curious to know just how important that Triangle herd was to the Tumbling H. He wanted to talk to Lennie Masters again, fit that Kansas Pacific letter into the pattern of the trouble there. He crossed the low hills at midday and paused to light a small fire and warm left-over beans and beef. Squatting there, he felt a sudden prickle down his back . . . it was the feeling of someone watching. He rose, kicked out the fire and mounted. He swung the roan around and looked back the way he had come.

The jumbled hills were empty and hot in the noon sun. He was getting jumpy, he thought. But the feeling that someone was following him nagged at his nerves.

It was mid-afternoon when he came through the low pass and hit the river.

The Timberlake came tumbling down out of the snow-capped San Miguels, cutting a deep chasm in the rocks at that point. It was a swift, narrow stream there, deep and turbulent. Three miles down-river the gorge planed out into the long valley and the river lost its power and widened to respectable proportions.

56

Larry rode to the edge of the gorge. The ledge fell fifty feet to the water below. Upstream, a spur of the chasm caused the rock to hook outward, away from the cutback in the gorge. Directly below him the water was comparatively still and deep . . . twenty yards from the ledge the current frothed whitely in its rush down to the valley.

Larry let his gaze move across the narrow chasm to the buildings of the Tumbling H, standing like toy blocks on a grassy saddle between timbered hills. Halliday had picked out a site for his spread with a cattleman's eyes. From the ranchhouse grassland ran to the river bottoms and behind him the foothills lifted to the San Miguels, the slopes of which offered ideal summer grazing.

Timber Pass was a notch in the sky behind the Tumbling H. It was the natural route into the long valley from the plains, and Brennan had the sudden conviction that a railroad building through the valley would come that way.

There was a fording on Halliday's map about four miles down-river. "We'll make it well before dark," he said, reaching over to scratch the roan's left ear.

The bullet went psst! past his face at that instant. The faint crack of a rifle hung like an exclamation point over the sullen booming of the river.

Larry jerked back on the reins, seeking to maneuver the roan away from the chasm. The animal stumbled on a slick spot and suddenly kneeled.

The second shot drew blood across Larry's arm. He went out of saddle on the lee side of the struggling animal, his Colt sliding into his hand. He heard the third slug thunk into the plunging roan, saw a faint wisp of smoke rise from the west shoulder of the pass.

He was on the edge of the chasm, with the fifty-foot drop at his back, and it was no place for leisurely observation. The roan was screaming with pain. Larry tried to get away from its crazed lunging, but the roan scrambled to its feet and unaccountably whirled toward him.

The animal's shoulder just grazed him as it went over the edge. The blow spun him around and off the ledge. He felt pain shoot through his right leg as he scraped an outjut of rock. Then he hit the pool to the left of the roan.

He hit the water in a sprawl, felt it slap his face, and he had only one thought: to protect himself from the thrashing hoofs of the maddened animal.

Something hit his shoulder a numbing blow while he was under water. Then he broke surface and felt the undercurrent tug at him, pulling him away from the slick gorge wall.

The roan was threshing around further away. Larry

57

searched the gorge wall for a crack to cling to. A barely submerged ledge offered temporary respite. He could barely move his left arm. His right leg pained him. Setting his teeth, he made the ledge and dragged his bruised body onto its temporary haven. . . .

Ira Johnson lined his sights on Larry and pulled trigger. His sudden cursing mingled with the report as the Texan unexplainably leaned forward in the saddle at the same instant. He knew he had missed and he hastily levered another load into the chamber and pulled trigger. He saw Larry jerk, then slide out of saddle just as he fired again, and in the blur of movement that followed he had no means of knowing he had missed again.

He saw the Texan and the roan suddenly disappear and a mental picture flashed into his head of a long drop and submerged rocks in the river bed.

Johnson spat out the piece of straw on which he had been chewing. He had been waiting fifteen minutes for the Texan to show up. Long ago he had guessed Larry would show up there. A rider coming through the low hills from the desert would naturally come through that pass to the river. He had guessed shrewdly, and only a fluke had kept him from making sure of the Texan.

He went back up the rocky slope to the timber where he had tied his cayuse and rode back to the ledge. The gorge wall jutted out slightly and he saw nothing in the water directly below. His eyes moved downstream. He caught a glimpse of the roan as it swirled in the grip of the strong current. Then it vanished around a rocky projection two hundred yards downstream.

Not entirely satisfied, Johnson rode to the downstream projection, dismounted and, rifle in hand, crawled down toward the water. From there he had a better look at the wall directly under the ledge. He saw nothing.

Returning to his cayuse, he mounted and rode downstream at a steady pace. He kept to the river until it widened, then swung south. He made for a low, rocky ridge that made a natural barrier at that end of the valley, and by time the sun dropped behind it he rode into the Ace of Spades ranchyard.

A chunky puncher slouched out of the bunkhouse and watched him pull up. He said: "Howdy, Ira," and the lanky killer asked: "Where's Charley?"

"In the house," the other said. "Plug's in there with him. An' those two Laredo gunslingers—Gans an' Crawford." He

58

looked at Johnson, curiosity in his eyes. "Looks like somethin's up, Ira."

Johnson nodded. "Yeah, somethin's up, Nate." He dismounted with the stiffness of a man who has been in the saddle a long time. "Take care of Nig, will yuh? I got to see Charley right away."

"Sure," Nate said. He took the black's bit and started for the corral. The black's head drooped as he walked and his hide was wet and steaming and a lacy white froth clung to his jaws. Nate wondered where Johnson had been.

Johnson walked wearily across the shadowed yard to the ranchhouse. His steps lacked spring, but he carried inside him the picture of Brennan dropping off that ledge into the Timberlake and it helped ease his aching frame.

Allison was sitting in a chair by a big stone fireplace. He had a glass of Scotch in his hand. There was a half filled bottle on the table in front of him. He turned and looked up when Johnson came in.

Plug Stewart, Allison's foreman, was sprawled out in a chair opposite the gambler. He was a burly man with enormous shoulders, a sandy, unkempt mustache and scowling features. He was smoking a cigar.

Joe Gans, and Dan Crawford, the Laredo gunsters, were standing by the fireplace. Gans had the thumb of his right hand hooked at the point where his gun belts crossed. He was a lean, quiet man with tawny hair, a small crescent scar on his pointed jaw, and icy gray eyes.

Crawford was a bulky man whose clothes always seemed too tight for him. He wore one gun, on his left thigh. He usually let Gans do the talking for him.

They were Allison's latest importations—and by far the deadliest.

Allison waved his free hand. "We've been waiting for you, Ira. Pour yourself a drink before you start talking."

Johnson crossed the room to the table and poured himself a liberal portion. He took the drink in two swallows, wiped his mouth with the back of his hand.

"I needed that," he said, then turned and looked at Allison, his eyes dark with satisfaction. "We won't have to worry about Brennan, Charley."

Allison straightened, his fingers tightening about his glass. "You sure, Ira?"

Johnson nodded. He found a chair and rolled himself a smoke as he talked, sketching in what had happened since he had left the Casino.

"He was headin' for the Tumblin' H when I got him,"

59

he finished. "I know I hit him with my second shot. Brennan went into the Timberlake from a fifty-foot drop. Even if he wasn't dead he couldn't have lasted in that current. Right about there is the worst stretch in the river—"

"All right, Johnson," Plug interrupted harshly, taking the cigar from his mouth. "So this Texan's out of the way. What about the herd? How many men with it?"

Johnson turned. He and Stewart didn't get along, and the burly foreman never made any attempt to keep the rasping enmity from his voice.

"Nine," he said coldly. "Nine—countin' the cook." He turned and talked to Allison. "The herd's bedded down in Lost Springs Canyon. They didn't even have a guard out when I got there. But Brennan must have told them to expect trouble, 'cause they had a lookout on the east entrance wall when I left."

Plug frowned. "If they're expectin' trouble they'll be hard to beat—"

"Yeah—if we had to get by that lookout," Johnson admitted. "But there's a joker in the setup which they don't know about. Sure, those Texans will be watchin' the canyon entrance. We'll hit 'em from behind. This way." He sketched the hidden passageway into the canyon, and a smile came to Allison's face.

"They'll never know what hit them," Johnson finished. He leaned back and looked coldly at Stewart.

Allison turned to the burly foreman. "This is all we wanted to know, Plug. Get the boys out of the bunkhouse and pull the raid tonight. You can make it before the sun comes up."

Plug got heavily to his feet. "I heard of that Triangle outfit," he said. "They got a tough reputation. I better get all the boys along on this, Charley." He put on his hat and turned, looking at the Laredo gunmen. "They comin' along?"

"No. I want Joe and Crawford with me. With the half-dozen boys in the Casino, we ought to handle any kickback that might come to town.". . .

Plug said: "You thinkin' of the Tumblin' H?"

Allison nodded. "This is the showdown, Plug. I can handle McVail. Joe can take care of Albright if that horse-faced deputy oversteps himself. And there's enough of us to take care of that Masters kid, if he comes to town looking for trouble."

Plug nodded. Johnson poured himself another drink before getting up.

"It's gonna be a long ride—we better get goin'. See you in a couple of days, Charley."

Chapter 11
The Law Moves

Sheriff Jim McVail opened the law office and hung his hat on the hook by his desk. It was early morning and Albright was not yet up. McVail was glad of this. He had come back to Douglas late the night before, and there were things on his mind he wanted to iron out before he talked to the lanky, keen-witted deputy.

He pulled his chair out from under the old roll-top and sat down, his rangy frame slumping against the chair back. He had been gone a week, and now there was impatience in him to get on with what he had to do.

He was a quiet, hard-eyed man in his late forties. Long ago he had come to accept the disfiguring scar on his left cheek—it was a long, puckered slash that twisted his face and gave him a sardonic, bitter look.

He had drifted into Douglas five years back, with a letter of recommendation from Sheriff Donahue in Cristobal and another from the governor of Kansas. Saunders, then sheriff in Douglas, took him on as a deputy, and when later Saunders resigned and left the valley McVail was appointed sheriff.

It had been five years of slowly gathering trouble, and now it was about to break. He felt caught in the impending storm and hampered by a decision he would soon have to make. It was not an easy one and he dreaded the outcome.

He shook off his worrisome thoughts and reached for the tobacco jar on his desk. He was filling his pipe when Carsons came in.

McVail turned and looked at the tall, spare banker, letting silence run between them, feeling the other's cold enmity. "Must be important to get you here this early, Mark," he finally said, waving his hand to a chair. "What's on yore mind?"

Carsons remained standing. "When did you get back?"

"Late last night," McVail replied, frowning. "Why?"

"Then yuh heard about Jeff being killed?"

"No," McVail sat up, surprised. "No, I didn't hear it. Who killed him?"

Carsons smiled with a thin cruel twist of his lips as if he wanted to savor the impact of his revelation on the lawman. "Bob Masters!"

61

The name went through McVail, stiffening him, bringing him up out of his chair. There was unbelief in him, and then anger came briefly to his eyes, narrowing his lids. "You sure of that, Mark?"

"I wouldn't be heah if I wasn't," Carsons said coldly. "That's why I'm glad yo're back. I wanted to see yo' first, befo' we took action. It's yo' job—but yo've been easy with that wild kid too long, McVail. Far too long. The honest citizens of Douglas are fed up with these killings, with all this trouble, and we're going to stop it, even if we have to—"

"Meanin' who by 'we'?" McVail interrupted coldly.

"Meaning the Citizens' Committee," Carsons snapped. "We're not going to stand for this sort of thing in Douglas. The time of the gunman is gone—irresponsible killers like young Masters have to be curbed."

"Why single out Masters?" McVail said. "You know as well as I do the type of men the Ace of Spades has been hirin' lately. Why not make a clean job of it?"

Carsons sneered. "I knew you'd try to cover up for the boy. Why I don't know. He's a wild, no-good orphan who should have been jailed long ago." He paused, watching the look on McVail's face, waiting to hear the lawman speak. Then, when the sheriff said nothing, he went on. "Sho'— I'll tell you why I'm singling out young Masters. Because Jeff was my friend and I want to see the man who killed him hung. That's why I'm going to see that Masters is brought to justice."

"Are you sure there isn't another reason?" McVail cut in harshly. "Isn't it because your daughter is in love with the boy?"

"Love—bah!" The banker spat. "Vanity is just a child. That young killer turned her head befo' I found out she was seeing him. But that's over with, McVail. I've settled that. Vanity's going away to school—in Virginia—as soon as I can get her packed."

"Just like that, eh?" McVail said, turning back to his desk and thumbing tobacco into his pipe. The scar on his face made him look particularly bitter in that moment. "Carsons," he said, turning and looking at the arrogant banker, "some day that sanctimonious, self-righteous cloak you got yoreself wrapped up in is going to smother you, just as it already has smothered every shred of humanity in you."

Carsons' lips curled. "You sound like a preacher—and I didn't come here to listen to a sermon." He pointed an arrogantly demanding finger at the lawman. "I want you to bring this Masters boy in, to have him stand trial for the killing of Halliday. If you don't, we will. And I won't be able to vouch for the temper of the committee members, or the swiftness with which they may decide to mete out justice."

"Justice?" McVail's tone was sarcastically bitter.

"Yes, McVail—justice." Carsons paused in the doorway and turned to deliver a parting ultimatum. "Better have that Masters boy in jail tonight, McVail—or the committee will ride tomorrow!"

Fifteen minutes after Carsons left, Albright came into the law office. He paused when he saw McVail at the desk, and a smile broke the grim line of his mouth. "Glad to see you back, Jim."

McVail said, "Thanks, Ben," in a preoccupied tone. Then he turned and looked at the deputy, his thoughts veiled behind the slow blue curl of smoke from his pipe. "Seems like things have been happening while I was gone."

Albright threw his hat carelessly on the bunk. "Yeah," he said shortly, frowning. "Halliday was killed two days ago, in the El Dorado."

"I heard about it," McVail said. "Carsons was just in here, giving me some plain talk. Threatened to use the Citizens' Committee if we don't get action." He took the pipe out of his mouth and watched Albright sprawl on the bunk, his back against the wall.

"Did Bob Masters kill Halliday?"

Albright shrugged. "Looks that way, Jim. The kid was up in Halliday's room just before Jeff was killed. Velie, the El Dorado night clerk, said he could hear them arguin' clear down into the lobby. When Bob came downstairs Velie noticed he was bleeding a little at the mouth, like he was cut. That got him curious, an' first chance he got he went upstairs. He found Jeff lyin' on the floor, an' ran out to get me."

The deputy reached in his pocket for the makings and talked while he rolled a smoke. "Jeff was clubbed to death, Jim. Don't see how anyone but Masters could have done it. I checked with Velie an' a couple of men who were in the lobby at the time it happened. They're sure no one went upstairs between the time Bob left an' when Velie found Jeff dead."

"How about the roomers in the El Dorado?"

"Questioned every one of them," Albright said. "If one of them killed Jeff I'll turn in my star tomorrow." He shook his head. "No one had any reason for killin' Jeff, outside of the Ace of Spades. I talked with Ned at the Timberlake stables an' he says Allison rode into Douglas about ten—two

63

hours after Jeff was killed—and he was plumb surprised to hear that Halliday was dead."

McVail said: "Reckon that's it, then." His voice had a strange quiver to it, and Albright had the funny feeling that McVail was acting like a trapped man, forced into doing something he did not like.

He watched McVail get up and reach for his hat. "Let's go get him," the sheriff said.

Albright straightened. "Masters?"

McVail nodded.

Albright came to his feet. "He's goin' to be a hard man to bring in, Jim." He frowned and unconsciously took a hitch at his gun belt. "Those Tumblin' H riders are behind him in this. I saw their foreman, Bill Tate, yesterday, an' he was pretty riled. He doesn't think Masters killed Jeff."

"I don't think the kid killed Halliday either," McVail cut in quietly. "But he's a hotheaded youngster with an itchy trigger finger an' primed for range war with the Ace of Spades. Jailin' him will be the best way to keep him out of trouble. I've got a few moves of my own to make, Ben, an' I don't want him forcin' my hand too soon."

Albright picked up his hat. "You find what you went after?"

McVail nodded. "Come on—I'll tell you on the way."

They left town, hit the river trail, and jogged north toward the Tumbling H. The morning sun glinted on the wide river. Albright listened, nodding silently here and there as McVail talked. "Wonder if Halliday knew?" he mused, glancing at McVail.

The sheriff shrugged. "That's why I want the kid out of the way, Ben," he said, but Albright had the curious feeling that there was another reason McVail wanted Masters out of the way—a deeper, more personal reason.

"Those cows Jeff was waitin' for," he said, changing the subject, "came in. If the rest of those Texans are as craggy as their trail boss we got more trouble, Jim."

McVail listened with frowning interest as Albright sketched in the events he had missed. "He left town yesterday, after killin' Trellis," the deputy concluded. "Charley tried to rig it so it would look like Brennan killed Nick without givin' him a chance . . . even sent the barkeep out to get me after it happened." The deputy's lips curled. "I'll be glad when we move in on him, Jim, an' that's just another reason why . . ."

"Where's Brennan now?"

"Out of town. Left word at the El Dorado he'd be back. I reckon he rode out to where he left the herd." Albright

64

looked at McVail. "We'll have to figger those Texans in any play we make," he said.

McVail shrugged. "We'll see," he said shortly.

They rode in silence after that. It was almost midday when they took the wagon road away from the river to the high saddle where the Tumbling H was located.

"... We give unto thee his spirit, may it rest in peace. ..."

Lennie Masters looked fixedly at the pine wood coffin being lowered into the grave.

Bob was at her side, lean and quiet, his arm touching hers, somehow drawing understanding from his sister. He had argued and rebelled against the softer temper of his uncle, but now that Jeff was gone he had a sense of personal loss, as had Lennie Masters.

They had grown up there on the Tumbling H ... they knew the game trails that led into the foothills, the pools where the steelheads lurked in the Timberlake ... and always, at the end of a day of play, there had been the welcome of the sprawling stone and log ranchhouse to come to and the sight of Jeff smoking contentedly on the veranda that faced down-valley and upon the Halliday acres.

Sam's voice droned on, reading from a pocket Bible. The words seemed to rake up all the accumulations of memory in Lennie, and she felt a lump rise in her throat.

Bob moved beside her and she felt the restlessness in this wild boy who was her brother, whom her mother had placed in Lennie's care.

Those had been Mary Masters' last words the night she died. "Take care of him, Lennie. You are all he has left now—take care of Bobby."

Bob was six when she died. He had come to her at the last hour, round-eyed and unknowing ... he had not cried even when they took him away and told him his mother had gone and would never return again. Lennie had gone into her room and cried. ...

The coming of Allison had broken the peace of the Tumbling H—Allison and his hard-eyed riders. Halliday had spent less and less time smoking contentedly on the veranda ... had become annoyed, then worried, and finally white-faced with anger and despair.

And now he was dead—killed by some assailant who had brutally clubbed him to death. ...

She looked at Bob, knowing his temper—then she thrust the thought from her, ashamed for having even momentarily entertained it.

They were on the small grassy knoll where another

grave, marked by a small headstone and carefully tended flowers, already preceded Jeff's. The knoll afforded a magnificent view of the river, and Mary Masters, who alive had often come there, had asked to be buried on that quiet spot.

On the far side of the grave the Tumbling H riders stood silent and awkwardly bowed. Sarah Luce, Sam's portly wife, stood next to Lennie.

Sam finished reading and closed his book. Two Tumbling H riders began to spade earth onto the coffin. Lennie stiffened slightly and Sarah placed a sympathetic hand on her arm.

Sam looked down at the earth falling on the coffin. "I knew Jeff for thirty years," he said. "Knew him when he was a young man with less than a hundred head of longhorn an' a dream about a ranch in the Timberlake—"

"Sorry to interrupt, folks. Just take it easy an' there won't be any trouble."

The voice intruded sharply into that sober gathering, stilling Sam's simple eulogy. Heads turned toward the ranch path.

Albright stood on a small rock commanding the knoll. He was tall and relaxed, the inevitable cigar stub in his mouth, a rifle held rather casually in his hands.

McVail came up the path, pushing into view, his face holding no expression other than his fixed, sardonic look. "Yo're under arrest, Bob," he said flatly. "For the murder of yore uncle, Jeff Halliday."

The youngster stiffened. Lennie felt the wildness surge up in him, sensed his sudden decision, and fear choked her.

Albright's rifle swung sharply, muzzling the half crouched kid. "Don't try to make a break, Bob. You're not fast enough to beat a .30-40 slug."

Across the half filled grave the Tumbling H men tensed, and violence flared up swiftly, blaspheming the quiet of Jeff's burial. One reckless move from Bob and the men across the grave would join him ... there would be more men to bury. ... Suddenly Lennie was sick of violence and death.

Her hand went out to her brother, felt him quiver beneath her restraining fingers. "No, Bob!" she cried. "No! Give him your gun and go peacefully!"

She saw him look at her, tense and rebellious ... she saw his lips whiten and the yellow flecks deepen in his eyes. ... Then he pulled away from her and relief came to Lennie, leaving her weak-kneed and spent.

McVail walked slowly into the clearing, holding his Colt in his hand. He walked up to Bob, reached out and lifted his gun from holster. Then he stepped back and jerked his head. "Come along. We'll saddle you a hoss at the ranch."

Sam came forward, facing McVail, shaking his head. "You know what yo're doin', McVail?"

The sheriff nodded. There was something between the two men, something unspoken, that was felt by the others. McVail's gray eyes held Sam's, as if challenging him, and finally Sam shrugged.

"Yo're makin' a bad mistake," he said tonelessly. "Bob didn't kill Jeff."

"That will come out in the trial," McVail said dispassionately. He turned to Bob and motioned with his Colt down the path. "Let's go."

"Some day I'm goin' to kill you!" Bob said, and his voice shook with the intensity of his feeling. "If it's the last thing I do, McVail—I'm goin' to kill you!"

The sheriff stiffened, his face hard and bitter in the morning light. Sam wet his lips.

Then Bob moved past him, walking quickly down the path to the Tumbling H, and McVail walked behind him.

Albright remained standing on the rock, his rifle holding the men around Jeff's grave. He waited until McVail's single shot told him the sheriff was waiting; then he stepped down, his voice level and warning. "Take it easy for a few minutes before following me. I've got a nervous trigger finger."

He backed down the path and disappeared around a bend. He ran back to where the sheriff and Bob waited in saddle. McVail held Albright's mount and waited until the deputy slid his rifle into his scabbard and got into saddle.

"Let's go," he said and didn't look at the tight-lipped kid riding between them as they hit the river trail and headed for Douglas.

Chapter 12
Out Of The River

Lennie walked slowly down the path to the ranchhouse. Sarah waddled along, trying to console her. "No jury will convict Bob on such flimsy evidence, Lennie. We'll see Lawyer Taylor tomorrow. He may even get Bob out on bail. . . ."

Socrates Sam walked behind them, preoccupied and worried, followed by the group of silent Tumbling H riders. They split in the yard, the men heading for the bunkhouse.

Sam followed Lennie and his wife up the stairs to the

wide veranda where Jeff used to wait for him. . . . The chair Jeff had built himself was tipped back against the wall.

Lennie sank down on the sofa, beaten. Sarah stood by, clasping her hands nervously, not saying anything.

Sam walked to the big stone fireplace and looked at the picture resting on the mantel. It was an old daguerreotype in a gilt frame.

It was a family group . . . a man in black broadcloth, ascetic-faced and black-mustached, sitting stiffly upright in a high-backed chair. At his left, one hand resting on the chair back, stood a sensitive-mouthed young woman; on the other a boy and a girl, aged three and five.

Sam turned and looked at Lennie. "What did yore mother tell you about yore father?"

Lennie looked up at him with surprise. "Very little," she said dully. "She never talked about him except to say he had been a good man and had been killed in an accident." Her eyes met his. "Why?"

Sam stood silent. "Nothin'," he finally answered, and turned away. "Come, Sarah."

The portly woman said: "Come with us, Lennie. You can stay in town with us."

The girl shook her head. "I want to be alone for a while. I want to think."

"Thinking, at this moment, is bad for you," the woman said. "And it won't change things."

Sam took her by the arm. "Come, Sarah." He looked down at Lennie, his eyes kind and understanding. "We'll be waitin' for you—later."

The girl shrugged. She walked to the door and watched Sam and his wife get into the buckboard and drive away. She stood there in the doorway until the buckboard became a speck on the river trail.

The sun was beginning to slant from the west. Saddled horses, stamping impatiently in front of the bunkhouse, drew her attention.

Bill Tate, Tumbling H foreman, came out of the bunkhouse and paused to slide a rifle into the scabbard on a rangy bay.

"Bill!" She came down the steps and crossed the yard, her voice halting him as he was about to swing to saddle. Behind him the rest of the Tumbling H men appeared, hard-lipped and silent. "Bill!" she said sharply. "Where are you going?"

"To town!" her foreman answered. He was a small, wiry man, sunburned and leathery, and he walked with a limp. He had blue eyes in a seamed, harsh face and she could tell by the coldness in them that there was going to be trouble. Tate had always sided with Bob against Jeff when Bob had counseled action against the Ace of Spades.

"Going to town won't help Bob!" she said. "I need you here!"

"Doin' what?" the Tumbling H foreman asked gruffly. "Mendin' harness?"

She caught at a straw. "The Texans will need help when they start driving the Triangle herd onto our range. There'll be more than enough work then."

Tate shook his head. "We're leavin', Lennie. The Tumblin' H is through. Allison's got us licked!"

She didn't believe it. "Bill!" she said. "You're quitting?"

He avoided her eyes. The others spread out and began to mount.

Tate looked at her. "Yeah, were quittin'," he said gruffly. and swung up into saddle.

She watched them ride out of the yard, then slowly walked back to the house. Benson, old and badly crippled, stood in the door of the harness shop. The screen door slammed in the quiet and Benson cursed softly. . . .

Brennan eased himself into the water, holding to the ledge with his fingers. Whoever had shot at him would probably investigate to make sure.

He twisted slowly, feeling the undercurrent pull at his legs. He couldn't be seen from directly above—the overhang took care of that. But if a man went downstream to where the gorge wall thrust out into the river. . . .

Larry's eyes caught a glimpse of the lanky figure climbing down the rocks. Taking a deep breath, he let himself go down into the water. The ledge was under three inches of water and his clinging fingers would not show even to a keen observer.

He remained under until he felt his lungs ache with strain. He came to the surface slowly, bending his head back so his nose came into view first. He expelled air slowly, took another deep breath, and sank down again.

The second time he came up he looked toward the wall. His ambusher was gone.

He held onto the ledge, getting back his breath. His right leg was getting numb. Larry turned and took stock of his predicament.

The river was less than sixty yards wide there. But it was impossible to buck the swift current, even if the opposite chasm wall should be scalable. Larry glanced at the gray rock over his head. There wasn't a crack offering a hand-hold within a dozen feet of him.

He was in a bad spot. He couldn't climb up and he couldn't swim across. . . .

His eyes swung back to the spur down which the killer had climbed. It rose in a series of broken steps to the gorge rim, and a man could make it from the river.

But it meant risking the swift current. For three hundred yards he'd have to ride the whitewater. And if he missed the spur there was little chance he could survive the battering rapids beyond.

Larry weighed his chances against the alternative of clinging to the cramped ledge, and decided there was no alternative. He took a last glance at the spur, then eased down into the water. He stroked easily through the still water until he hit the current . . . then the whitewater lapped against his face and the current took hold of him roughly and swung him around. He didn't fight it. He rode it downstream, his body tense with fear of submerged rocks, the booming roar of the torrent filling his ears.

He shook spray out of his eyes in time to see that he was being carried away from the spur and the realization galvanized him into making an effort. He fought the current, seeking to keep to the edge of it. The rock wall loomed up before he was aware of it.

His right hand reached out and closed over a jutting knob. The current tore him loose. He dragged along the rocks, his fingers clawing, seeking purchase. The skin was torn from his fingers, but he found a handhold and desperation gave him strength.

The river roared in his ears, mocking him, seeming to overpower him with its noise. The current slammed him roughly against the rocks. Pain shot up from a bruised shin. But he hung on.

His toes found a crack in the wall and it gave him leverage against the current. He clung like a crab in a crevice, getting his strength back. Then slowly he shifted his right hand to a projection above his head and pulled himself out of the river.

It took him fifteen minutes to climb that fifty-foot wall to the top. He found a small rock and sat down, breathing harshly. The quivering of his strained muscles stopped and anger came to him, setting his lips in a thin line.

The sun was hot in his face as he got up and limped back along the gorge to the spot where he and the roan had gone over. He picked up the tracks of the killer's horse and followed them up the slope.

Scraggly timber peppered the hillside. Three hundred

yards from the ledge Larry found where his ambusher had crouched by the side of a huge boulder that jutted out of the earth. A cigarette butt lay to one side of the boot marks.

Larry let the obvious fact sink into him. The killer had been waiting for him. As no one could possibly have known he'd hit the river at that spot, it meant that he had been followed. Followed all the way to Lost Springs Canyon where the killer had evidently waited overnight for him to start back.

Larry grudgingly gave the man credit for some good tracking and shrewd guesswork.

Once he had struck across the low foothills rimming the Mesa Seco sinks, the natural contour of the land would bring him through that pass to the river. The killer had known this and hurried ahead to lie in wait.

Larry tried to pin down his glimpse of the man who had climbed down the spur . . . tried to compare that lanky figure with the killer who had sat with Allison across from him in the Casino.

This had become personal, this trouble he had sought to avoid—and Allison had pulled him into it. The gambler would probably attempt to carry out a raid on the Triangle herd to keep it from being delivered to the Tumbling H, and Larry was glad he had ridden out to warn the boys.

In the meantime he had to get to the Tumbling H, where he could borrow a cayuse to take him to town. The ranch was only three miles away as the crow flew, but to Brennan it meant going downriver until he could find a fordable spot. . . .

Four miles below the ledge where he and the roan had been targeted, the river emerged from the gorge and widened, flowing less rapidly through low wooded banks. Larry limped to the water's edge and judged the current.

If he was going to make the Tumbling H by nightfall he'd have to make his crossing there.

He took off his boots and fastened them under his belt. He had lost his Colt in the fall and for a moment he thought of discarding his cartridge belt. He finally decided against it. Wading into the river until it reached his armpits, he swam across.

He crawled out on the opposite bank one hundred and fifty yards downstream. He felt winded and chilled. He dumped water from his boots, wrung out his socks, his pants and his shirt. Then he put them on again and walked stiffly up the bank to the river trail.

The sun had dropped behind the hills when Brennan limped into the Tumbling H ranchyard.

Tired as he was, he could still appreciate the layout that had been Halliday's life work. There was a rambling stone and log ranchhouse shadowed by tall, evenly spaced poplars on the north and east. Across the yard was the bunkhouse and the harness and blacksmith shops, and behind them a corral and a small barn where saddle horses were kept.

Beyond this a pole fence enclosed a pasture that ran part way up the slope to the north. A score of milk cows grazed contentedly near the fence facing the ranch.

Larry paused in the middle of the yard, sensing the unusual quiet, the air of desertion that seemed to linger there. The bunkhouse was unlighted, its door open to his gaze. Frowning, Larry started for the ranchhouse. Someone was at home there, for there was a light in the windows.

A man moved out of the shadows of the harness shop, his voice thin and querulous. "Where you headed, stranger?"

Larry paused and swung around. Twilight lingered in the yard. The man with the shotgun shuffled slowly toward him. He was an old codger, stove up and unable to ride. His kind usually hung around a ranch, making themselves useful chopping kindling for the cook and doing odd jobs.

"I'm Brennan," Larry said. "Trail boss from Texas."

Benson paused. His gaze took in the Texan's condition—he was hatless, empty-holstered and bruised—and slowly he lowered the shotgun. "Looks like you need a change of clothes," he said gruffly.

"I had a bit of trouble crossin' the river," Larry admitted.

"Come along," Benson said. "I'll get yuh some o' Big Tim's clothes. They'll be a mite large but they're dry."

Larry followed him into the bunkhouse. The absence of other Tumbling H riders puzzled him.

"Where's the rest of the crew?" he inquired casually.

Benson scraped a match and lighted an oil lamp on a table in the middle of the room. He turned and looked at Larry, his seamed face emotionless.

"Left," he replied laconically.

Larry sat on a bunk and pulled off his boots. He watched Benson rummage around in a locker at the far end of the room and then came back with socks, pants, shirt and long underwear.

"Hereyar," the old-timer said.

He sat on the bunk facing Larry and watched the big Texan peel to the skin and get into the clothes he had brought him.

"Boys left coupla hours ago," he broke the silence. "Right after McVail an' Albright come an' arrested Bob Masters."

Larry stood up and tightened his belt around Tim's pants.

72

They were a little roomy in the waist. "You mean they quit?"

Benson shrugged. "They made it look that way—to Lennie. But I'm figgerin' they headed for town—an' trouble!"

Larry walked to the bunkhouse door, tightening his cartridge belt at his waist. Dusk was fast blurring outlines in the yard.

"You say Miss Masters is home?"

Benson came up beside him. "Yeah." He looked into the yard, and added softly: "She hasn't been out of the house since the boys left."

Larry left the old man and crossed the yard. The shadows were thick against the house and the poplars stood up tall and majestic, making a windbreak on the north.

There were flowerbeds in front of the house and the thought came to the Texan that this was what he would have liked . . . a place like this and a woman waiting for him.

He knocked on the door, and waited—and after a long silence Lennie's voice came: "Come in."

Chapter 13

Third Man To Die

Brennan opened the door and stepped inside the long living room. Lennie Masters was sitting at a table. A book was opened in front of her, but Larry could tell by the blank expression on her face that she had not been reading.

She looked at him now, without interest. "I'm glad to see you," she said.

"Thank you," Brennan said dryly. He indicated his clothes. "I ran into a bit of trouble crossin' the river an' one of yore men dug these up for me."

She sat there, beaten and alone, trying to keep some shreds of composure about her, but she wanted to cry. All the things that had made up her life were gone, or about to go.

Larry stood in the half-shadows by the door. He was big and solid and there was a quiet strength about him that drew her. All her life, after her mother died, she had been tied with the responsibilities of her brother—and now that responsibility weighed heavily upon her.

Almost desperately now she wanted to put her trust in someone, lay her responsibility in stronger hands. . . .

Larry felt her helplessness. He walked to her, faced her across the table. The shaded lamp left his face in semi-shadow.

"I heard what happened," he said softly. "Heard that Mc-Vail jailed yore brother—an' that yore men left you."

She nodded. He stood silent, and after a while she said: "I'm through fighting. All I want is to get Bob out of jail. I'm going to sell what's left of the ranch."

"I never saw a better layout," he interrupted quietly. "It's worth fightin' for."

She smiled bitterly. "In two more days, without cows on the range, the ranch will be taken over by the bank and auctioned off. I have no real choice."

Larry frowned. "I should have Barstow's answer tomorrow. It'll only take six or seven hours to get that Triangle herd on Tumblin' H grass."

"If Barstow says to go ahead—" she reminded him.

He was silent. She was right. He should have been more explicit when he had wired the Triangle boss—explained the situation. But he hadn't known it himself—and now it was too late. He couldn't promise her anything, and he knew it.

"Just what is the situation?" he asked. "Why did Jeff let himself get caught in such a deal?"

The girl shrugged. "Two years ago Jeff borrowed money from the bank to build a dam across Crazy Horse Creek on our lower range. Carsons inserted a clause that authorized him to call in the loan if at any time Uncle Jeff failed to show cows on the range. Uncle was never keen on legal matters, and Mark Carsons is a friend of ours. I understand Uncle Jeff was advised it was there merely to reassure the bank's depositors—and Jeff could not foresee, of course, the trouble that followed."

Larry nodded. "Then Allison's men started to make trouble," he said quietly.

"We could never prove they were Ace of Spades riders who ran off our cattle," she said. "There was talk of rustlers operating out of Grizzly Hollow. Before we woke up to what was happening most of our cattle were gone. We sold most of what was left to meet the loan, but it wasn't enough. Carsons was nice enough to extend payment last year, but this year he warned Uncle Jeff he would have to call in the amount of the loan. Uncle asked him for more time and Carsons gave him until the end of this month. That was when Uncle Jeff wrote to John Barstow."

Larry nodded. "It was a long drive," he said. "A thousand miles. We got here as fast as we could."

"I don't blame you," the girl said. "It's not your fight."

"No," Larry admitted, "we didn't come looking for trouble. But I got into it the night I rode into Douglas." He reached into his pocket and pulled out the letter he had taken from Bates. It was wet and the ink had smeared, but it was still legible.

"A bum named Bates had this on him when he came up to my room in the El Dorado," he said. "He took me for Jeff and died without knowin' he was talkin' to the wrong man. This is what he wanted to give yore uncle."

The girl took the letter and read it, then looked up at Larry, puzzled and a little troubled. "The Kansas Pacific? What does it mean?"

"Power!" Larry said bluntly. "Money—which is the same thing. Whoever owns land over which the railroad will build will make a fortune."

She looked at the address again. "Mark Carsons. How did Bates get hold of this letter?"

"Probably out of Allison's desk," Larry said. "He worked in the Casino an' mebbe he was a nosy human. He might have gone through Allison's desk one night and seen the letter. He probably got the idea yore uncle might like to know that the Kansas Pacific was coming through Timberlake Valley an' be willin' to pay for it."

Color was coming into Lennie's face. "But it's addressed to Carsons," she said. "How could Allison have gotten possession of it?"

Larry said: "I wouldn't know."

He turned as a Chinese cook shuffled into the room and announced: "Supper ready, Missee Lennie."

The girl hesitated. Then she turned and asked: "Will you join me—Larry?"

They ate in silence, and took their coffee back to the living room. The girl was moody and depressed. Larry rolled a cigarette with the papers and tobacco he found in a jar on the mantel. The picture caught his eye—he looked at it steadily—then he turned as Lennie crossed the room toward him.

"The family picture," she said. "That was taken in Memphis just before Father died. We came to the Tumbling H shortly after."

The mantel clock bonged softly, its eight strokes fading into the stillness.

Larry straightened. "I better be gettin' on," he said. "Barstow's wire may have come in. I'd like to borrow a hoss an' "—his hand brushed down past his empty holster and

75

he frowned—"I could use a gun. Mebbe I could use yore uncle's until I get another one to replace the one I lost."

"You expecting trouble?"

He shrugged. "I like to be ready to meet it."

"Uncle Jeff quit wearing a gun five years ago," Lennie said. "He was getting on in years and said it only invited trouble."

"The invitations have already been sent out," Larry said dryly. "I got formal notice a few hours ago, when one of Allison's men took a couple of shots at me across the river. It wasn't his fault he didn't make the invitation a funeral notice."

She frowned at his grim levity, not understanding how he could joke about trouble.

"I'll get Uncle Jeff's gun for you," she said.

He finished his cigarette while waiting, occasionally glancing at the framed picture and the man who had not lived to see his children grow up.

Lennie Masters came back with a long-barreled Dragoon model Colt .45. Larry felt the heft of it, finding its balance as it lay in his hand. He let it slide into his holster, drew it in a quick, eye-baffling motion and was satisfied.

"I'll get Benson to cut you out a horse," Lennie said. They crossed the yard to the bunkhouse. The oldster was sitting on a bench in front of the shack, smoking a pipe.

"Mister Brennan's going to town," she said. "Give him his pick of what's in the corral—he can use Uncle Jeff's saddle. And"—she made a sudden decision—"saddle Prince for me. I've decided to go to town myself tonight."

She turned to Larry. "I'll get dressed." She went back into the house.

Benson rose. "Saddles're in the harness shop," he said briefly. Larry followed the limping oldster, conscious of the stiffness in his own leg, the lesser bruises he had suffered in the river.

Benson lighted a lantern and indicated a saddle to Larry. The Texan gathered up extra gear, then reached out and said: "Here, I'll take it," as Benson labored with another saddle.

Benson nodded appreciation and they went to the corral. A half-moon was pushing up over the hills across the river. Larry sat the saddles on the top pole of the corral, draped extra gear across them, and followed Benson inside.

The crippled oldster had taken a riata from one of the saddles and was shaking out a loop. He nodded to the small bunch of horses crowding the far end of the enclosure.

"Prince's the palomino," he said. "The small one next to the gray."

"I'll take the black," Larry said—"the one with the spot of white on its nose."

Benson glanced up at him. "That's Ebony. Best cayuse in the remuda. But he's stubborn an' he'll fight yuh every time."

"I like a fighter," Larry replied.

He waited by the gate while Benson walked slowly toward the wary animals. They grew restless at his approach. Ebony snorted and edged away, prancing along the far end of the corral. The palomino turned its head and seemed to divine it was Benson's objective. It stood still, it's cream hide ghostly in the pale moonlight.

Benson paused. He was close enough for a cast, but the gray was shouldering the smaller palomino, not giving him an opening. Benson made a sudden move. The palomino wheeled and trotted toward the far side of the corral. The others followed, keeping bunched up.

Benson swore. He followed them, forced the palomino to break from the others and crowd along the corral bars. Benson shuffled after it. It came loping along the bars toward Larry. The Texan stepped out in front of it and the palomino wheeled. Benson, shuffling right behind, had a clean shot.

His noose settled around the palomino's neck. The animal fought briefly, then gave up. It had fought and submitted innumerable times before and it was rope-broken.

Benson led the animal to the gate and Larry helped him saddle it.

"How long has Allison owned the Ace of Spades?" he asked Benson.

"Four years. Used to belong to the Terry brothers—never was much. Up in poor range country under Hurricane Ledge. The Terry boys ran a few cows an' broke horses for a livin'."

Larry was shaking out a loop and keeping his eyes on Ebony. Benson finished tightening the cinches on Prince. "Allison bought 'em out under mighty queer circumstances. An' right after that we began to have trouble."

Larry nodded. He walked away from Benson, keeping his eyes on the black. Corral-wise, the black kept close to the others crowding the bars.

Larry turned his back and walked a few steps away. The bunch wheeled and started back for the spot under the shade tree where they had been before the interruption.

Larry wheeled, and caught the black in the open. His

77

wrist flipped the noose and it settled over the black's arched neck.

The next few minutes were a brief battle between horse and man. Larry managed to snub his end of the rope to one of the corral posts, and talking softly, coaxingly, walked up to the quivering animal.

The black eyed him belligerently, but calmed down as he slid a reassuring hand along its flank and patted him gently. Larry had a way with horses.

Benson looked admiringly at him when he led the black to the gate. "Outside of Bob, there ain't a man on the ranch who kin get that close to Ebony."

Larry saddled and swung aboard. The black uncorked itself for a workout that didn't last long. He was pretty docile by the time Lennie Masters came down the ranchhouse steps and crossed the yard to them.

"I'll be staying with the Luces," she told Benson. "Take care of things until I get back."

They left the ranch and took the river road to Douglas. The moon painted the hills with a silver light and the river wound like a ribbon in the night.

They didn't have much to say, and it was late when they entered Douglas. They stabled the horses at the Timberlake stalls, and Larry walked with Lennie to the Luce cottage.

He said good night at the gate and watched her walk to the door and knock. After a long wait someone came to the door. It was dark and Larry couldn't tell if it was Sam or his wife, but Lennie disappeared inside. Larry turned and walked to El Dorado.

Velie, the night clerk, was dozing when Larry entered. He woke with a start when the trail boss reached across the desk and tapped him on the shoulder.

"Oh!" he said sourly. "It's you."

Brennan frowned. "Were you expectin' someone else?"

The clerk shrugged. "I thought you left for good."

"You an' the day clerk ought to get together some time," Larry interrupted. "Did a wire come in for me?"

The clerk turned and looked into a pigeonhole. "Nope," he said irritably. "Not a thing."

Larry felt like reaching out and shaking the sour-faced clerk until his teeth rattled, but he restrained himself. "The room still vacant?" he asked brusquely.

The clerk nodded. "Far as I know." He turned and looked in a cigar box. "Thought I had the key in here," he said, frowning.

"Never mind." Larry said, turning away. "I left the door unlocked."

He walked through the deserted lobby and went upstairs. He was halfway down the narrow hall when he noticed that the door to his room was ajar. Light from inside made a yellow bar on the warped board flooring.

He quickened his pace and was frowning as he pushed the door open.

Saber swung around, an expression of annoyance on his swarthy face. The annoyance faded into shocked surprise.

The Ace of Spades gunman had been bending over the bed, going through Brennan's bag. He took a step away from it now, his voice expelling "Brennan!" with a harsh, clipped sound.

He drew with the name on his lips.

Halliday's Dragoon leaped into Brennan's fist. Saber's gun had barely cleared leather when Larry's slug hit him in the chest. He fell backward against the bed. His Colt went off, sending a slug into the wall. He turned convulsively and slid off the bed and lay sprawled on the floor.

The Texan walked to him. The broken spur on the swarthy man's boot caught his eye. He had seen that boot and spur at close quarters two nights before, while bending over Bates' body.

Holstering his Colt, Larry sat down on the bed. The room, he thought wryly, was jinxed.

This was the third man to die in it since he had come to Douglas.

Chapter 14

Death Prowls At Night

The night clerk appeared in the doorway. He looked at the body by the bed, then at Larry and, mumbling something unintelligible, beat a hasty retreat.

Larry felt in his shirt pocket for tobacco before he remembered he was out. The tie strings of a Bull Durham sack dangled from Saber's pocket and he leaned over and confiscated it. He was halfway through his cigarette when boots clumped heavily up the stairs and came toward his room.

McVail came into the room, frowning. Ben Albright shuffled in behind him. The deputy flicked a glance at the Texan, dropped his gaze to Saber, and raised an eyebrow. He eased back against the wall by the open door and let the sheriff take over.

79

Velie, the hotel clerk, hovered in the hallway, flanked by several sleepy-eyed spectators.

The sheriff let his glance rest briefly on the body, then shifted his attention to Larry. Albright filled in drawlingly: "That's the Texas trail boss—Brennan. This in his room. Same one Jeff an' Bates died in."

"Must be contagious," McVail said humorlessly. His eyes searched Larry's hard face. "What was Saber doing up here?"

"Takin' over," the Texan replied levelly. "I found him goin' through my belongin's like he owned them. When I walked in he went for his gun. . . ."

Saber was sprawled at the foot of the bed, his gun still clenched in his fist. The Texan's roll was spread out on the bed. McVail walked to the dead man and pried the gun from clenched fingers. He sniffed at the muzzle, swung the chamber out and frowned at the fired cartridge.

Saber considered himself a badman," the sheriff said musingly. He looked at Brennan, his lips quirking. "So you're Brennan?"

Larry looked at Albright, sensing trouble. "Yeah—I'm Brennan."

"Heaved Nick Trellis through a window, and killed him later in the Casino," the sheriff said, still in the low, musing tone. "Now it's Saber."

He spun the chamber of Saber's Colt, clicked it back in place, and thumbed back the spiked hammer. Then he turned and flipped the muzzle up, lining it abruptly on the Texan.

"You're too handy with a gun, Brennan!" he said coldly. "We'll have to keep you bottled up for a spell!"

The move caught Brennan by surprise. He had killed Saber in self-defense—the thing would have been plain even to a ten year old. He tensed, his voice going sour. "Was this polecat a friend of yours, McVail?"

The sheriff didn't answer. Albright stepped away from the wall. "Shuck that gun belt, Brennan," he said softly.

Larry got up slowly, knowing he could not beat the gun in the sheriff's hand, knowing he'd have to give in, but hating it. "All right," he said harshly. "You hold the ace cards." He unbuckled his belt and let it fall at his feet.

"Step away from it!" McVail ordered. He waited until Brennan obeyed, then nodded to his deputy. "Take his belt, Ben." He stepped back and motioned toward the door. "You go first," he said to Larry. "And don't try to make a break for it. It won't get you anywhere but a box at Socrates Sam's."

The small group crowding the doorway gave way as they went out. Larry walked down the stairs and out through the lobby. On the walk outside, McVail and Albright flanked him. The sheriff kept Saber's gun in his hand, held flat against his thigh.

"This way, Brennan!"

They crossed the street and went north two blocks and stopped before a one-story building with an iron-barred window. Albright rapped on the door, and after a while the bolt slid back and a keen-faced man with buck teeth opened the door. He had a double-barreled shotgun in his hands.

McVail said: "Thanks, Kenny," and the man nodded as he stepped back and replaced the gun in the wall rack. "Any time, Jim—any time you need help," he said quickly. He looked at Larry. "This the feller who did the shooting?"

McVail nodded and walked to the desk and tossed Saber's gun on it. Albright heeled the door shut and said: "Saber finally got what he's been lookin' for, Kenny. Another customer for Socrates Sam."

"Saber!" Kenny said sharply. "The Ace of Spades gunslinger?"

McVail nodded as he came back and Kenny turned to look at Brennan with new interest.

Albright said "Get some sleep, Kenny. I'm stayin' in tonight."

McVail opened a door to the left of his desk and motioned Larry down a short corridor that ended in a blank wall. Facing the corridor were several iron-barred cells.

He unlocked a cell door and waited. Larry walked grimly past him into a bare room with a small barred window high up in the back wall. An Army cot was set up under it. McVail locked the door and Albright said "Pleasant dreams, Brennan."

Larry watched them walk away. He heard McVail say to the horse-faced deputy: "I'll see you first thing in the morning. I don't expect trouble from the Tumbling H tonight, but if anything happens don't try to buck it alone. You know where to find me."

The door closed on the office and darkness blotted out the corridor. Moonlight wedged in through the small window, curling about the barred cell partition with ghostly fingers.

Someone creaked on the cot in the next cell; then Bob Masters' voice came, bitterly amused: "Who'd you throw through a window this time, Brennan?"

Larry turned and walked to the bars separating him from

81

the next cell. His eyes were adjusting themselves to the darkness. He saw the wiry youngster sitting on his cot, smoking a cigarette. The kid got up and walked to the bars, looking in at Larry. His cigarette flared as he dragged in smoke, lighting up his stubbled, wild face with its quick red light.

"I just killed a polecat named Saber," Larry said. "Found him goin' through my warbag when I got back to the El Dorado."

Masters stiffened. "Saber!"

Larry reached into his pocket for the makings. "Yeah. Friend of yourn?"

Bob sneered. "No one who works for the Ace of Spades is a friend of mine." He turned and started pacing, like an impatient cat. He prowled around his cell and came back to where Larry was waiting.

"You say McVail jailed you for killin' Saber in self-defense?" He was close up against the bars and the moonlight brushed his lean, taut face. "I've known all along McVail was in with Allison. This proves it!" His hands clenched around the bars and his voice was as soft as tearing silk.

"I've hated McVail ever since he stopped me from gunnin' Allison, a year ago—right after Allison's gunnies made their big raid on Tumblin' H stock. Jeff an' my sister backed him up. The law, they said—McVail's the law!" The kid's lips curled back against his teeth. "Whose law, Brennan—whose law?"

The Texan was silent, understanding the kid's bitter hate. "I don't know," he said.

"I'll tell you!" the youngster grated. "Allison's law!" He relaxed his grip on the bars and the intensity faded from his face. "But I've got a joker hidden up my sleeve, too," he said softly. "I'm gettin' out of here, Brennan. Soon. An' when I do I'm gonna kill McVail!"

Larry shook his head. "Killin' McVail won't stop Allison. It won't stop you an' yore sister from losin' the Tumblin' H."

The kid walked around the cot and came back. "What are you goin' to do with that herd?" he growled. "Those cows are the only thing that can save us. What are you goin' to do with 'em, Brennan?"

"Turn them over to the Tumblin' H—soon as I get Barstow's okay," Larry said. Then, remembering Lennie's decision to sell, he added: "Yore sister's in town—stayin' with the Luces. She'll probably be around to see you in the mornin'. She's goin' to sell the Tumblin' H. That's a mistake, kid. Tell her to hold on a little longer."

Young Masters paused in his pacing He came to the barred partition and looked at Brennan, as if making up his mind about the big Texan. Finally he said: "I just ran out of tobacco, Brennan. How about the makin's?"

Larry smiled as he handed his Bull Durham sack through the bars.

Beefy Burns grunted a little at the exertion expended to reach the top of the canyon cliff.

"Yo're gettin' soft," Chuck Wallis chuckled, coming out to meet him. "Yo're puffin' like one of them steam engines tryin' to make the grade at Willow Junction."

Burns ignored the gibe. He turned and looked into the eastern sky, trying to detect a crack of light. A chill wind whipped about his legs.

"Dawn in another hour, Chuck," he growled. "See anythin' out there?"

Chuck shook his head. "Hope Larry gets back today with orders," he said. "I got a yearnin' to hit the home trail for Texas."

Burns grunted. He watched the slim Triangle puncher merge into the shadows hugging the cliff wall. Then he turned and took up a position on the ledge where he could survey the moonlighted approaches to the canyon mouth.

He had a three-hour watch, and it would be light when Red came up to relieve him. He settled himself with his back against the ledge wall, his rifle across his knees, and rolled himself a smoke.

The moon painted the hills in the east with ghostly light. The approaches to the canyon were level and the sparse vegetation cast small blotches of inky shadow.

Burns scraped a match on the rock by his side and lighted his cigarette. It looked like a dull watch. . . .

Chuck walked to the Triangle camp. His trailmates were asleep, rolled up in blankets by the embers of a fire. The remuda stirred sleepily among the cottonwoods by the spring.

The slim puncher yawned, stretched, and unrolled his blanket. It was good to be getting some sleep.

A shadow stirred by the wagon and he whirled, his Colt sliding into his hand. "Hello!" he said sharply. "Who is it?"

"Me," Johnny said, walking toward him.

"What'n hell you doin', prowlin' around like that?" demanded Chuck. "Wanta get shot?"

Johnny said: "Can't sleep. Guess I'll take a pasear around. Maybe I'll go out an' relieve Carp."

Chuck slid his colt back into its sheath and unbuckled his gun belt. "Better let him know yo're comin', kid," he warned. "Carp's the kind who shoots first."

Johnny nodded. "I'll let him know."

Chuck watched the kid move toward the horses. Johnny

83

vanished among the shadows around the chuck wagon, and Chuck grinned at the sudden thought that came to him. Hank slept under the wagon with one ear cocked. If the kid tried to swipe something out of Hank's larder there would be hell to pay.

He rolled up in his blankets with that thought in his head, and two minutes later he was asleep. . . .

Burns yawned. He got up and walked to the edge of the ledge. The moon had gone down and the pre-dawn dark lay over the Mesa Seco badlands.

He had seen nothing in the hour that had passed since relieving Chuck. He felt cold and heavy-lidded and he cursed the necessity of being there.

The ledge was just below the main level of the cliff top. He climbed up and stretched cramped muscles. A thin line of light was cracking the edge of the sky in the east. Burns grunted and reached into his pocket for tobacco. . . .

The shadowy figure came toward him, looming out of the darkness of the mesa top. Burns stiffened, his rifle swinging around to cover the man. "That you, Red?"

A red flare answered him. Burns felt the shock of the slug in his chest, and he pulled the trigger of his rifle as he staggered back, a vast surprise blanketing his mind.

The shadowy figure fired again. He came forward at a run and stood over the Triangle puncher. Burns moved and the killer sneered as he emptied his Colt into the man at his feet.

The shots stabbed down into the canyon camp with their abrupt alarm. Triangle men rolled out of blankets, sleepy-eyed and confused, to meet the charge of shadowy riders that came shooting into camp.

Chuck got to his feet in time to get a bullet in his shoulder. He made a dive for the chuck wagon and got another slug in his leg before he rolled in beside Hank.

Duke shot twice at gun flares, cursed the bullet that creased his arm, and was heading for the wagon when the slug sent him sprawling against the wagon's high rear wheel. The collision knocked him out, and Hank pulled his limp figure in beside Chuck.

Carp stood his ground, his rifle spitting. A half-dozen guns targeted him and he fell, riddled.

Red pumped lead into the shadowy riders that swept through camp. He was hit twice, the last time in the chest. One of the riders wheeled back and deliberately rode his horse over the wounded puncher.

Hank bellowed an earthy oath as he let go with a blast of his shotgun. The rider tipped forward over his suddenly pain-maddened cayuse's neck. Another rider pulled up alongside and caught the animal's reins.

Jim was staggering toward the wagon. Hank crawled out to help him. A rider loomed up an he swung the shotgun around. The bullet raked across his back, pulling him off balance, and the shotgun blast went up into the air. The rider wheeled and blasted Hank's tottering figure.

Hank sank down beside Jim's still figure.

Plug Stewart wheeled his mount. "Let's go!" he ordered. The raiders swung in behind him. A voice said: "Samovar's hit pretty bad—"

"Stay with him," the Ace of Spades foreman ordered. "Head for the valley. We'll be comin' along with the cows. . . ."

The Triangle cattle were fidgety. They moved restlessly as the mounted raiders turned them up-canyon. Daylight was moving swiftly across the sky, paling the stars.

From the shadows along the western wall "Parson" Johnny watched the cattle string past. He waited until cows and riders faded into the grayness filling the canyon before following on foot.

Down at the Triangle camp there was no sound save the soft murmer of the springs. . . .

Chapter 15

The Cows Are Gone

McVail entered the office and found Albright shaving. The deputy turned and said: "Yo're early, Jim. Didn't expect you till after breakfast."

"Had breakfast," McVail said. He walked to the desk and threw his hat on it. "Quiet last night, Ben?"

"As the inside of a church." Albright finished shaving, rinsed his face and wiped it dry. "Tate's an old-timer, Jim," he said, turning to the cot where he had discarded his gun belt. "Used to ride up the trail an' shoot up Abilene when he was younger. But I reckon he's cooled off a bit."

McVail settled himself in his chair. "Those Tumbling H boys didn't come into town for nothing, Ben. They're looking for trouble. Long as they're in town we'll have to keep on our toes. I don't want 'em breaking young Masters out of here."

"They won't!" Albright growled. He buckled his belt about

his lean waist and shifted the holster against his leg. "I'm goin' out for some ham an' eggs, Jim."

McVail nodded. "We'll talk to Brennan when you get back."

Ten minutes after the deputy had left Vanity Carsons knocked timidly on the door. He opened it and stepped aside to let her in.

"I'd like to see Bob," she said quickly. "I'm leaving tomorrow for St. Louis, and I would like to see Bob before I go."

There were dark circles under her eyes, as if she had been sleeping badly, and McVail felt sorry for her.

"Does yore father know you've been coming to see young Masters?"

"No." Her dark eyes glanced up at him, pleading for understanding. "Can I see him?"

McVail walked to the desk and took a bunch of keys from a nail. "Sure," he said kindly. He opened the door and let her precede him into the corridor.

Larry was sitting on a cot. He got up and walked to the bars. "How long you gonna keep me here, Sheriff?"

McVail ignored him and opened the door to Bob's cell. The youngster was tensed on his cot, eyeing the sheriff with bitter hate. Vanity turned, a tremulous smile conveying her gratitude to the scarred lawman.

McVail let her in. Then he locked the door behind her and walked back to his office. He filled his pipe and leaned back in his chair, letting his decision take shape in him. By the time he got up and let Vanity Carson out, he knew what he was going to do.

Albright came in a few minutes later, chewing on a stub of cigar. "Allison just rode in," he said, throwing his hat on his cot. "He had those two Laredo gunslingers with him— Crawford an' Gans!"

McVail nodded. "Get that Texan in here, Ben. I want to talk to him."

Albright walked down the corridor to Larry's cell and unlocked the door. "McVail wants to see you, Brennan."

Larry got to his feet. "Nice of McVail," he said grimly. He was burning with a slow anger as he followed the deputy to the office.

McVail looked up as Brennan came into the room. He had the Texan's gun belt and holstered Colt on the desk in front of him. He picked it up and handed it to Brennan.

Larry took it and buckled it about his flat waist. "Glad you thought it over, McVail," he said coldly. "I was beginnin' to lose all respect for the law in Douglas."

86

McVail shrugged. "Long as you have some left," he observed dryly, "it'll make me happy."

"Am I free to go?"

McVail nodded. "After you answer a few questions."

Larry rubbed his chin stubble. "I'm hungry an' I need a shave. Make it short, McVail!"

Albright scowled and came away from the wall. "Yo're too damn cocky for yore own good, Brennan."

McVail waved his deputy to silence.

"You've been in trouble since you came to Douglas," he said frowning. "You'll have to learn no man is bigger than the law here. You stay out of trouble from now on or I'll see that you take up permanent quarters in that cell you just vacated. Get that straight, Brennan!"

Larry's lips curled. "Just to keep the record straight," he said angrily, "I didn't come lookin' for trouble. I had a herd to deliver to Halliday—"

"And you found Halliday dead!" McVail cut in. "What did Bates want that night?"

Larry frowned. "What are you gettin' at?"

McVail came to his feet. "Bates had something he was going to turn over to Jeff. Something important enough to have a man follow him to the El Dorado for it. What was it, Brennan?"

"That's what Saber must have been lookin' for last night," Albright added. "Did he find it?"

Larry smiled. "No. Saber didn't find it." He reached into his pocket and tossed the Kansas Pacific letter on McVail's desk. "That's what Bates wanted to give to Halliday."

McVail picked it up and read it, his scarred face showing no emotion. Then he folded it and put it in his pocket.

Larry said: "You through?"

McVail shrugged. "Just keep out of trouble while yo're in town," he said shortly.

Brennan took a hitch at his belt. "I'm not guaranteein' anythin'," he said flatly. "I'm beginnin' to feel that kid you got back there is right. 'Whose law?' he said. 'Allison's law!' No. McVail—I'm not guaranteein' anythin'. I got a herd south of here—cows we trailed a thousand miles for Jeff. If anythin' happens to those cows while I'm in town, I'm not goin' to wait for the law."

He turned as the door opened and Lennie Masters came into the office. Socrates Sam was right behind her.

The girl said. "Larry! I heard you had been jailed."

"Yeah," the Texan said. "But McVail decided it was a mistake."

87

Lennie looked past him to the sheriff and color whipped up into her face.

"How much is Allison paying you, Sheriff?" she said contemptuously.

McVail flushed. "No more than you are, Miss Masters."

Sam, moving in behind her, said quickly: "We came in to see Bob."

It was intended to change the subject, to dissipate the girl's anger. But Lennie's eyes were blazing, as if long withheld emotions had finally come to the surface in her.

"I hope you're satisfied, McVail. Someone murdered Uncle Halliday, and you cover up your inefficiency and bungling by arresting my brother. It's in keeping with your entire policy, isn't it? All the time Jeff was coming to you for help you put him off with promises and excuses. He believed you were backing him, even when we lost the last of our stock. He listened to you when you advised him not to bring in men who could oppose Allison's hired killers. You said that would mean range war and you weren't going to let that happen here. Well, you've had your way, McVail! Halliday's dead and my brother is in your jail, charged with his murder. If that's what you wanted, you should be a proud man today. But I'll always remember you as a small man, hiding his incompetence and his thievery behind a lawman's badge!"

It was a long speech—a contemptuously bitter denunciation. McVail took it in silence, his disfigured features showing no emotion, only his eyes revealing a strange hurt.

"I'm sorry that's the way you see it, Miss Masters," he said mildly. He turned away from her and walked to the window. His shoulders were square and stiff against the sunlight coming in. He said, without looking back: "See that Sam and Miss Masters get to see Bob, Ben."

Albright nodded grimly. He looked as if he wanted to say something, but he restrained himself and chewed savagely on his cigar. "This way!" he snapped.

Anger still burned in Lennie's face. She hesitated in the doorway and looked back to Brennan. "When shall I see you again, Larry?"

"Soon as I check on that wire from Barstow," Larry said. "It should be in this mornin'."

She nodded and followed Albright down the corridor. Sam shuffled to the door, then looked back at the sheriff.

"She was mad, McVail," he said, speaking to the lawman's back. His tone had a note of apology. "She didn't mean what she said."

McVail did not turn. Sam looked at him a moment longer,

88

then shrugged and walked down the corridor to Bob's cell.

Brennan frowned. There was something in McVail's attitude that spoke of a hurt that reached deep, a scar more disfiguring that the one on his face.

Shrugging, the Texan turned away. . . .

The day clerk at El Dorado gulped when he saw Larry approach. The Texan propped his elbow on the counter and jabbed a finger at the man. "If I find a body in that room this mornin', I'll sue tne hotel for operatin' under false pretenses!"

The clerk grinned weakly. "Has been a lot of trouble hasn't there?"

"That wire come for me?"

The clerk shook his head, and Larry scowled. He crossed the lobby and went upstairs to his room. Saber's body had been removed, but his roll lay spread out on the bed as he had left it.

Larry opened the window and looked down on the back stairs. The sun slanted into the yard and a breeze fluttered the faded curtains against his face.

If the Masters kid hadn't killed Jeff, then who had? One of Allison's gunnies, perhaps. The killer could have come up those back stairs, waited until Bob had gone out, then come through the window into the hallway and thence into Jeff's room. But Jeff would have put up some kind of a fight, would have yelled or made enough noise to attract attention. It was hardly likely he would have let in anyone he didn't know. . . .

Brennan went back and sat on the bed, thinking of the night he had slept there. He had not wanted to get mixed up in the trouble. But Allison had forced a decision on him.

He got up and paced. What was holding up Barstow's answer? He felt an urgency now to see this thing through. There was little time left, Lennie had said, before Carsons would call in the loan that would mean foreclosure and then auction.

He stopped in front of the dresser mirror and looked at himself. His hair was disheveled and his hard face had a three-day whisker crop. He winced, remembering that Lennie Masters had seen him that way.

What in hell? he asked himself suddenly. What does it matter if that girl did see you like this? What does she mean to you?

He sat down to figure it out. All right, he said to himself. So you've come a thousand miles to stick yore neck into trouble. You don't have to stay. In another hour or two you should get the wire. No matter what the old man's answer is you can be on yore way back to Texas in another day. Are you going to stay because of that girl?

He got up and walked to the wash basin on the stand by the dresser. He washed and changed into clean clothes. He combed his hair and then went down and had a late breakfast in the hotel dining room. He had promised Lennie he would see her as soon as he got word from Barstow, but he wanted to look right when he did.

He stopped for a shave at Tony's, bought himself a hat in a store on the same block, and turned in for a drink in the Preston House.

A group of men in range clothes took up one end of the long bar. Larry wondered if they were the Tumbling H riders who had come to town. He would have joined them, but they looked clannish, and he had nothing to say to them anyway. Not until he got that wire.

He had his drink and walked out. He crossed the street and made his way to the telegraph office on Lodestone Avenue.

There was a man at the key. Larry waited, listening to the staccato message going out over the wire. When the man finished Larry said: "I'm Brennan. Expectin' a wire from Texas—"

The operator tilted his green eyeshade and looked up at him. "Jerry just went out to the El Dorado with it. Came in five minutes ago."

Larry said: "Thanks," and walked out. He was passing Sam's Funeral Parlors when Lennie said: "I wouldn't have recognized you if it wasn't for your walk, Mister Brennan. You always seem as though you were going some place in a hurry." She smiled. "Is it that important?"

He took off his hat, conscious of its newness. "Nothin' will ever be that important," he said gravely. She was standing in Sam's doorway, and there was a question in her eyes as they met his, as if she were wondering what lay behind his answer. Then she looked away and sought refuge in a change of subject.

"Have you received your wire?"

"It was Larry in the sheriff's office," he said, keeping his eyes on her. "People who don't like me call me Brennan, an' the mister is plumb superfluous."

"All right then," she laughed. "Have you received that wire—Larry?"

He smiled. "It should be waitin' for me at the El Dordo."

"I'll come with you," Lennie said. She turned and called to Sam inside. "Tell Sarah I'll be late for dinner."

90

She turned, hooking her arm in Larry's "There's still time, if Barstow's answer is favorable."

She paused, feeling the Texan's arm stiffen. Brennan was staring up the street where a sorrel horse with a sagging rider in saddle was coming at a run.

"Duke!" Larry said harshly. "It's Duke!"

He left Lennie and began to run toward the winded animal. Duke was heading for El Dorado. Larry reached him as the Triangle puncher pulled the sorrel to halt by the hotel rail.

Duke folded over the horn, fighting his weakness. His shoulder had been roughly bandaged, but blood made a wide ragged circle in the bindings. Larry eased the puncher out of saddle.

"What happened?" he asked sharply, but the answer was in Duke's contorted face before the puncher spoke.

"Raided! Beefy, Carp and Red are dead! Johnny's missing! The others are shot up!" Duke's face tightened, fighting the pain he felt. "Damn it, Larry—the cows are gone. ..."

Chapter 16

The Tumbling H Rides

Larry carried the slim puncher into El Dorado and set him down in one of the stuffed chairs by the potted palms. Lennie pushed through the crowd that circled them and touched Larry's arm. Her face was white and questioning. "Who is he?"

"Duke," Larry said grimly. "One of the men I left with the herd. There's been trouble."

"They hit us from behind!" Duke interrupted harshly. "They were already in the canyon when they hit us, Larry— damn it, don't ask me how they got by Beefy. But they did! Caught us asleep."

"Take it easy!" Larry said. "I'll get you a doc."

"I'll go," Lennie said quickly. "I'll get Doctor Stillwell. His office is a little way down the block." She turned and pushed through the crowd.

Brennan singled out a pop-eyed individual staring at Duke. "You—get a shot of whiskey from the bar!"

The man shuffled off and Larry turned back to the Triangle puncher. Someone called: "Brennan!" and the Texan looked around impatiently. The day clerk came through the watching men and handed him the telegram. "Come for you a few

91

minutes ago," he said. He looked down at Duke with curious eyes.

Larry glanced at Barstow's reply.

Dear Larry:
   Sorry about Jeff. Use your own judgment concerning the cows. Wire me later.

Brennan crumpled the message in his fist. Barstow's message had come too late!

The pop-eyed man came back with the glass of whiskey. The shot seemed to revive Duke. He sat up and pushed hair out of his eyes. "I left Chuck and Jim in camp," he said thickly. "They were too shot up to ride. Hank's got a creased head and a broken arm—he's taking care of them until we get a doctor out there."

Brennan felt a tightness pull at his cheeks. Allison had made good his threat, but if he thought Brennan had been bluffing about a comeback he was soon to find out different.

"What happened to Johnny?"

Duke shook his head. "Chuck saw him prowling around, right after he came back to camp. Beefy relieved him on the cliff just before daylight. There was a moon last night, and Chuck swears no riders could have come within miles of the canyon without his seeing them, Larry. But less than an hour later they hit us. Johnny had relieved Carp. I know, because Carp was in Camp when he was killed. I rode out to where the herd had been grazing before coming to town—and there was no sign of the kid; dead or alive."

He stopped and glanced at the girl pushing through the crowd, the doctor right behind her.

Doctor Stillwell was a small, busy man with kind eyes and a bushy gray beard. He took charge without a word.

"Not too bad," he said, after exposing the wound. "Bullet ripped through shoulder muscles and chipped a piece of bone. Lost some blood, didn't you, feller?"

Duke nodded. He winced as the doctor swabbed the ugly bullet hole with a strong antiseptic. The medico bandaged the wound with swift efficiency. "That'll do it," he said briskly, snapping his black bag shut. "You'll be as good as new in a couple of weeks. However, better take it easy for a few days."

Duke sat up. "Take it easy hell!" He saw Lennie looking at him and flushed apologetically. "I'm sorry, Miss Masters. I assume you are Lennie Masters?"

She nodded. "I've heard men swear before," she said, smiling faintly. "Sometimes it's a help."

"I wish it were," Duke said bitterly. "But it won't change

92

things—it won't bring back Carp, Burns and Red. It won't bring back the herd we trailed all the way from Texas for you."

"It's all right," Lennie said. She said it as though it didn't matter. She had given up hope of saving the Tumbling H the day McVail arrested her brother.

"No!" Larry said harshly. He took her by the shoulders. "It's not all right, Lennie. We're goin' to fight! Understand? Fight! We're not givin' up now. I'm not takin' this raid sittin' down, waitin' for the law to move, the way Jeff did. *I know who's behind it!* Mebbe I won't have proof to show the law, but to hell with McVail an' his law anyway! We'll settle this the way Halliday should have done long ago—the only way men like Allison an' his riders can understand!"

"How?" the girl asked hopelessly. "How, Larry? There's only you and Duke."

"There's yore men!" he snapped. "I heard they were in town, itchin' for a fight."

"They quit yesterday," she reminded him.

"Good men don't quit!" Larry said. "There must have been a reason for their walkin' out on you. Where do they usually hang out in town?"

Hope came into the girl's eyes, kindled by the earnestness in the grim Texan. "The Preston House on Lodestone Avenue."

"Who's yore foreman?"

"Bill Tate. He's been with the ranch almost as long as Uncle Jeff."

Duke got to his feet. "Wait," he said tightly. "Wait for me. I'm coming with you!"

Bill Tate cut the poker deck and watched Lefty Harris deal. He chewed steadily on the wad of cut plug, leaning aside occasionally to let loose a liquid stream into a nearby spittoon. He eyed his cards gloomily.

"Dang it, Lefty—every time yuh deal I wind up tryin' to draw to an inside straight." He discarded three cards, morosely stared at the remaining two.

The Tumbling H men were grouped around a table at the far end of the Preston House bar. Counting Sancho, the bunkhouse cook, there were seven of them.

Slim Nichols glanced at his hand and tossed it into the discards. "Ain't had openers in three hands," he complained. He looked at Tate. "Either Albright or that badge-worshippin' freightline manager, Kenny, sleep in," he said. "If we wait until McVail leaves we won't have him on our hands when we walk in."

Tate shrugged. "The explosion at the Casino will create so

much confusion it'll be a cinch to break the kid out of jail."

Big Tim leaned back in his chair and grinned. He had the huge, muscular arms of a blacksmith and the grin of a ten year old who had just placed a firecracker under his maiden aunt's rocking chair.

"Allison's sure goin' to be surprised," he chuckled, "when that charge blows the back of the Casino plumb through the roof. I got her fused an' planted under the Casino's rear stairs. . . ."

"You sure no one saw yuh this mornin'?" growled Tate.

"Naw—the town was asleep. I tell yuh she's ready for tonight, Bill."

Lefty said: "Raise yuh two bits, Tim."

Tate looked at his cards again and scowled. "I'm droppin' out." He tossed his hands into the discards and stretched. "Joints are gettin' a mite stiff these days."

Lefty chuckled. "Age sure is creepin' up on yuh, Pop."

Bill was sixty, but he didn't show it. He did as much riding as any man on the Tumbling H, despite an old leg wound that caused him to limp when he walked. He had been brought up in harder times than the present. He had trailed cows into Dodge and Abilene when crossing the plains country was a hazardous venture of unknown and treacherous river crossings and raiding Indians.

"Long as it don't kick me in the face, son," he replied. He got to his feet, took a look at Lefty's hand, shook his head and walked to the bar. "Shot of Old Crow," he said to the bartender.

He toyed with his glass, thinking of more peaceful days on the Tumbling H. The boys at the table, like himself, had been with Halliday a long time. The newcomers had drifted away at the first signs of trouble.

It had started on a small scale. Tally books began to show no natural increase. The next year marked five hundred cows less than the year before.

Old Halliday had scowled. "We had a hard winter, Bill," he growled, "but not that hard. Spring calves alone should have more than made up for the natural loss." He had looked at his foreman, frowning and a little worried. "Damn it, Bill—cows just don't disappear."

"Not less'n those nesters up at Grissly Holler have been ridin' our range nights, Jeff. An' I don't like the looks of that outfit that took over the Ace of Spades. We're gonna have trouble, looks like. . . ."

It had been prophetic, that remark. The rustling had become night raids on a large scale . . . several Tumbling H men had been shot. There had been clashes with Ace of

Spades range riders—hard-eyed men who rode with rifles across their saddles.

It had been hard to obtain proof, to get their hands on evidence that would stand up in a court of law. Jeff had gone to Douglas to see McVail, and McVail had warned him not to start an open war.

Tate sneered now at the recollection. There had been a time when a cowman made his own laws and enforced them with the guns of his riders. Tate still adhered to that code. He was not a patient man, and his reasoning was usually direct. The trouble had started when Allison took over the Ace of Spades, and to Tate that was proof enough. Like young Masters, he had wanted to gather the Tumbling H men behind him and ride out to the enemy ranch for a showdown. . . .

He drank his whiskey and slowly poured out another. Halliday had paid a price for his caution, but Allison was going to find there was a kickback left in the Tumbling H. He nodded grimly to himself. The Tumbling H had been shoved around long enough. . . .

He saw Lennie in the big bar mirror as he set his glass down on the bar. She pushed through the swinging doors and paused, looking swiftly around the room. Behind her stepped a big, hard-eyed man Tate guessed was Brennan, and a slim, handsome chap with his left arm in a sling.

He turned around as she saw him and came across the room. "Mornin', Lennie," he said. His eyes met Larry's. "This the Triangle trail boss?"

Lennie said: "Yes, Larry Brennan—this is my foreman, Bill Tate."

"Duke," Larry said, nodding to the puncher at his side.

"Howdy," Tate replied. "You lookin' for me?"

Larry said: "Where can we talk?"

Tate waved an arm toward his Tumbling H mates. They walked to the table and the old foreman pulled a chair from a corner and offered it to Lennie. He remained standing.

"What's on yore mind, Brennan?"

Brennan looked at the men seated around the poker table. They were leaning back, not looking at Lennie. Between them they had evidently decided on a course of action and would not be easily persuaded to follow him. But getting back that Triangle herd, or as much of it as they could, came first. Those cows could save the Tumbling H. . . .

"Reckon you all know I came up the trail with cows for Halliday," he said bluntly. "When I got here Jeff was dead."

Tate's voice was dry. "That why you held up delivery?"

"I had my orders," Larry answered. "Deliver to Halliday. What would you have done, Tate?"

The Tumbling H foreman shrugged.

"It's still not too late," Lennie said. "If you'll help Brennan—"

Tate frowned. "Help?"

"The Triangle herd was raided last night," Larry said bluntly. "Three of my men were killed. The others are shot up. Duke here just rode in with the news."

Tate scowled. "What do you want us to do? Waste time tryin' to round 'em up for yuh?"

"Not for me!" Larry snapped. "For the Tumblin' H!"

Tate glanced at his riders. He had his own plans, and he didn't want to be put off. "No," he said shortly.

Duke looked at Brennan. "Come on, Larry," he said thickly. "Let's get out of here."

Lennie Masters got up and stood beside the big Texan. Her voice was low, without censure. "I told you they had quit, Larry. They no longer ride for the Tumbling H."

Lefty threw his cards on the table. "Wait a minnit," he growled. "Where did you say you were holdin' those cows?"

"In Lost Springs Canyon, where Halliday told us to."

"There's something very strange about that raid," Duke added. "We had a lookout on the cliff and there was a moon last night. We were sure no raiders could get in without being seen. But they did. Not only that they completely surprised us. And the strangest trick of the night was that they didn't haze the cows *out* of the canyon. They drove them up into it—and vanished."

Lefty looked at his companions, then up at his scowling foreman. "I'm for ridin' with Brennan," he said. "This other play we had in mind can wait. I've got a hunch we'll find out how our cows disappeared, too."

Nichols shrugged. "Count me in."

"All right," Tate muttered reluctantly. "We're ridin'. We'll meet you in front of the El Dorado in ten minutes."

Chapter 17

The Law Lays Down An Ultimatum

McVail looked up as Kenny came into the office. He had sent Albright for the bucktoothed men who ran the Douglas end of the Simmons Freight Company. Kenny was capable, honest, and not easily bluffed. And he didn't mind doing a little work for the law.

"Sorry to have to call you in again," McVail said, smiling. The scar twisted his face into a grim leer, but his eyes backed his smile with little crinkles. "Some day the county commissioners will authorize another deputy, but until they do I'll have to call on you for help."

"It's all right," Kenny said heartily. "Glad to do it."

McVail put on his hat. He took some papers out of his desk drawer and thrust them into his coat pocket. He took a hitch at his double gun belts, slid his right hand down over the slick walnut butt of a .45, and said: "Albright and I have a couple of calls to make. I don't want to leave the office unguarded—not while we have the Masters kid in there. There's too much talk of a lynching going around, and there's more than half a dozen Tumbling H men in town waiting for a chance to break the kid out of here."

Kenny shrugged. "I heard talk about the lynching. But we won't have trouble with the Tumbling H. I saw them ride past my office, heading out of town, just before Ben showed up. That big Texan you had in here last night— Brennan—he was with them. There was Doc Stillwell and the Masters girl, too—and a stranger with an arm in a sling. . . ."

McVail frowned. Albright said: "Somethin's up, Jim. I better look into it."

The sheriff shook his head. "We'll do that later. There's something else I have to do first."

They went to the Casino. The gambling hall was deserted at that morning hour. Two men idled at the bar; another was playing solitaire at a table under the balcony.

Barney stopped wiping glasses and came over to them when McVail crooked a finger at him.

"Where's Allison?"

"Upstairs," Barney said. He watched the sheriff and Albright swing away from the bar without further conversation. He stared after them, a little worried, then shifted his glance to the man playing solitaire. The gunman had stopped playing. . . .

Albright knew the door to Allison's office. He shoved it open and followed McVail inside, kicking the door shut behind him and lining up beside it, his back against the wall, his hand on the heel of his Colt.

Allison was behind his desk, a heavy mahogany affair that went with the plush furniture, the wine-colored drapes, the deep imported rug.

Gans was standing up, a cigarette between his thin lips.

He had been listening to Allison—they both turned when the door opened—and Allison stiffened, a watchful glint sliding into his gray eyes.

He crooked his lips about a fat cigar. "Mornin', McVail," he said. He deliberately ignored Albright. "What brings you around so early in the day?"

McVail looked Gans over with cold disrespect before bringing his gaze around to Allison. "I've come to give you notice," he said. His voice had a level quality, and a finality as definite as falling granite.

Allison straightened up. "Notice?"

"You're packing and leaving Douglas," McVail said bluntly. "I'm leaving you until tomorrow night to settle your affairs and leave Timberlake Valley."

Allison looked at McVail, surprise slackening his lips about his cigar. Then he leaned back in his chair and laughed. "You're crazy," he stated flatly.

McVail smiled, that twisted, bitter smile of his. He looked at Gans. The Laredo gunman was sneering.

"You're leaving tomorrow night, before sunset," he repeated coldly. "And that goes for all your hired gunslingers, Charley. Or I'll fill my jail with the lot of you."

Allison crushed out his cigar on the tray in front of him and came to his feet. "You're running a damn poor bluff, McVail!" he snapped. "I don't know what's behind this, but even the law can't go around ordering honest citizens out of town—"

"Since when," McVail sneered, "have you been honest, Charley?"

Allison's lips tightened. "What are you getting at, McVail?"

"There's a longer and a more legal way of doing it," the sheriff said. "I could get the Terry boys down here and have them testify how they came to sell you the Ace of Spades. I could, if I have to, show the court proof that your men rustled Tumbling H stock, ran it across the Mesa Seco country and road-branded with a HA for quick sale to the northern mining camps. I could do all that—but I won't. I'm giving you a break. I'm giving you a chance to pull your freight—"

The door opened abruptly and a big, bulky man in range clothes came barging in. He paused when he saw McVail. This was Crawford, the other Laredo gunman who had come to Timberlake with Joe Gans to join the Ace of Spades.

Albright leaned over and palmed the door shut without taking his right hand from his gun. He looked at Crawford.

"If yuh got any ideas, shuck 'em," he said coldly. "Seein' yuh invited yoreself in this, get over by the window an' listen."

Crawford shot a quick glance at Gans. The slim gunman wore a poker face; the smoke from his cigarette drifted up past his eyes. Crawford hesitated.

Albright snapped: "Git movin'!"

The gunman looked him over with flat insolence. Then, getting no signal from either Gans or Allison, he shrugged and walked to the window.

Allison's brittle laugh speared through the tension in the room. "I'm calling your bluff, McVail. We're not leaving!"

McVail turned to him, his eyes coldly uncompromising. "I never bluff, Charley," he said levelly. "You ought to know that from way back."

Charley sneered. "Sure, I know you, McVail. From way back. Back to the days when we were teamed up and played the suckers on the river boats. You weren't a lawman then, giving orders. You were McVail, who never gave a sucker a break. Memphis McVail—"

"You've got a good memory," McVail interrupted dryly. "It will make it easier for you to remember this—get out by sunset tomorrow!"

There was a silence in the room, heavy with the threat of violence. McVail turned and started for the door.

Allison's brittle voice stopped him.

"There's a lot more I'm remembering—*Masters!*"

He was smiling as the sheriff turned—he was playing his hole card and he knew he had McVail beaten.

"I knew that would bring you around, Jim," he sneered, slurring McVail's name with insolent familiarity. "You didn't think I knew, did you? But I found out from Diamond Kate what your real name was. Found out the night she died aboard the 'Mississippi Queen.' Jim Masters, who deserted a wife and two kids to run after Diamond Kate, queen of the riverboat entertainers!"

McVail's face was white, twisted with bitter shame. Albright was stiff by the door.

"What are you going to do now?" Allison taunted. "Still going to run me out of Douglas?"

The sheriff was silent, his lips pressed tightly against the pain of searing memory. Gans was smiling faintly and Crawford wore a scowl on his broad face.

"*Get out!*" Allison snapped, riding his advantage. "Get back to your offce—and take that horsefaced deputy with you, Masters! Or I'll spread the story from Douglas to Grizzly Hollow."

He stopped as McVail walked up to the desk and faced him across its wide surface. There was murder in the sheriff's twisted face and it spoke in his voice.

"The story had to be told sometime, Charley. But it'll be the last story you'll ever tell. I'll be around to attend to that—tomorrow!"

The silence was thick and choked as he turned and walked back to the door. "Come on, Ben—let's go!"

Carsons was in his private office in the bank when McVail and Albright entered. He looked up at them, surprise and apprehension mingling on his face. Then he put a smile of welcome on his thin lips and said: "Mawning, Sheriff. How are yuh, Ben?"

The lawman nodded.

Carsons pushed back from his desk and motioned to a cigar box in front of him. "Take a couple, Jim. You too, Ben." His voice was genial. "Glad to see yuh finally got down to business. Jailing Bob Masters—"

McVail walked silently to him and tossed a letter on the desk. He ignored the cigar box. Albright remained by the door, the cigar stub in his mouth, not saying anything.

Carsons frowned. He looked at the letter without picking it up. Then he looked up at the silent sheriff, surprise in his voice. "I lost that letter about two weeks ago, Jim. Where did yuh find it?"

"I didn't find it," the sheriff said. "I got it from Brennan. Brennan took it from Whiskey Bates, the same night Halliday was murdered."

Carson's gray eyebrows arched. "Are you trying to implicate me in Jeff's killing, Sheriff?"

The sheriff leaned over and tapped the watersmeared envelope with a blunt finger. "I don't have to," he said quietly. "This does it for me."

"Why?" Carsons said sharply. "What are you trying to prove, McVail?"

"That you've known for some time the Kansas Pacific was going to build through Timberlake," the sheriff said.

"So I have," Carsons cut in brusquely. "That was my business, McVail!"

"And Allison's!" McVail snapped. "That's why Allison had this letter and Bates came across it in his snooping. He stole it and went up to the El Dorado, not knowing Jeff was dead. He knew Halliday would be interested in finding out about this Kansas Pacific deal. The Tumbling H stands across the only logical way into the valley!"

Carsons wet his lips. His eyes were suddenly on the defensive. "Jeff was my friend, McVail. I loaned him money when he needed it—extended his loans when he couldn't meet payments."

"It was a nice setup," McVail interrupted. "You loaned him money, and Allison broke him. You worked with Charley to get control of the Tumbling H."

"You can't prove anything!" Carsons snarled. He came halfway out of his chair, his goatee jerking. "You're trying to run a bluff."

"That'the second time today I've been accused of that," McVail said. "I'm getting tired of it."

The banker sank back in his chair. "You can't prove anything," he repeated.

"I wouldn't bet on it," the sheriff said. "It took me a long time to dig up the facts, Mark—to find out about that HA brand you filed up in Coahuilla County so that Allison's men could make a quick change to that iron on the hides of the Tumbling H cows they rustled. Cows they later ran north to Poke, Sabine and other mining camps. . . ."

Carsons wet his lips. The arrogance was stripped from him, and he looked old and gray. "What do you want me to do?" he said, almost in a whisper.

"You're going to break up this phony Citizens' Committee," McVail said. "And you're going to cancel that Tumbling H loan. I don't care if that money has to come out of your pocket—cancel it."

"What about Allison?"

"Allison will be out of Timberlake Valley by tomorrow night—or he'll be dead!" the sheriff said.

Carsons bowed his head. "All right, Jim," he said softly. He kept staring down at his desk and he didn't look up as McVail and Albright left.

Kenny said: "Didn't take you too long McVail," as the sheriff and Albright came into the office.

The sheriff shrugged. He walked to his desk, hung his hat on a hook beside it, and said: "Thanks, Kenny."

The freight-line manager hesitated, trying to read something in the faces of the two men. They were two of a kind —sheriff and deputy. Quiet, deliberate—they worked smoothly together.

He said: "Socrates was in here a while back, looking for you, Jim."

The sheriff made no comment.

Albright walked to the cot and sprawled his lanky frame on it. He said: "Don't work too hard, Kenny," as the buck-toothed man shrugged and started for the door.

101

There was a long silence after the door closed; then Albright said: "So that's why you never clamped down on the kid, Jim?"

The sheriff sat in his chair, facing the wall. He didn't turn. "It's a long and not a pleasant story, Ben." His voice sounded tired. "I left my wife and kids in Memphis after we'd been married six years. Couldn't stand the monotony of a clerking job. . . too restless.

"Mary was a frail sort of woman. She didn't want to leave town . . . didn't want to come West with me. So I finally chucked the whole thing and took to the riverboats. I met Charley in St. Louis. He was known as Silk Allison. We teamed up for a while, working the side-wheelers up and down the river. We didn't get along too well, and finally we split up over a show girl."

"Diamond Kate?"

The sheriff turned around. "You knew her?"

"Heard of her." Albright reached into his pocket for his sack of Bull Durham and rolled himself a smoke.

"There was trouble one night," McVail went on, "the same night I got this." He lifted a hand to the ugly scar that twisted his features. "Diamond Kate was shot—I never found out who did it—the Missouri Queen set afire. . . ."

He was looking back now, reliving the scene. "River pirates. . . ."

He was silent for a moment, then shook off the bitter memory. "I drifted West and lost touch with Charley. Finally the restlessness wore off. I went back to Memphis to see Mary. She was gone. I found out she had come out here to live with her brother, Jeff Halliday. I drifted some, not caring much what happened, and finally came to Timberlake.

"Mary had been dead for more than ten years. Halliday had never seen me—he wouldn't have recognized me anyway, with this. The kids had grown up. I decided I'd hang around, keep an eye on them."

"Then Charley showed up in Douglas." The sheriff got up and walked to the window and looked out. "And then I knew there was going to be trouble. . . ."

Albright finished his cigarette without speaking.

Sam came in, his corncob stuck in his mouth. He glanced at Albright, then walked to McVail. "Hear the news, Jim?"

McVail turned. "What news?"

"The Triangle herd's been raided. One of the Texas trail riders rode in with a slug in his shoulder and a story. Doc Stillwell fixed him up and a half-hour later he rode out of town with Brennan and the Tumbling H boys. Lennie went with them."

He stopped and looked questioningly at McVail's stony face, then shifted his gaze to Albright. "What are you going to do about it, McVail?"

"Nothing," the sheriff answered. "Nothing—now. . . ."

Chapter 18

Parson Johnny Kills A Man

The sun speared down over the rough slants beyond the mesa, starting the heat waves shimmering in the bottoms. A hot wind blew into the hidden valley from the badlands, siphoning through the break in the towering walls.

Ira Johnson pulled his bay aside to let a gaunt-flanked Triangle steer lumber by. He watched it go down to the river's edge and begin to drink, his eyes resting briefly on the bony hindquarters. Trail lean, these cows would not bring much of a price in the mining camps north of the Diamond Heads.

The animal turned away from the river and joined the rest of the Triangle herd grazed in the shade along the bottoms. Most of them browsed under the trees that dipped their foliage over the crystal clear stream.

There was little danger of their scattering too far. The feed away from the river was poor and the sun hot. They'd be bunched up and easy to get moving in the morning, Johnson thought. But he was glad he wasn't staying with the drive. It was thirty miles across a blistering lava bed to the next water. . . .

He felt his weariness as he swung the bay toward the camp a quarter of a mile downstream. Smoke made a lazy curl against the dark green of an oak grove, and Johnson's thoughts leaped ahead to coffee and a few hours' sleep in the welcome shade.

Except for brief periods, he had been in saddle since he had followed Brennan out of Douglas, and it was beginning to tell on him.

The bay quickened its pace, sharing Johnson's desire for relief from the blistering sun. They cut around a bend in the stream and the north wall of the valley came into view. On the other side of that wall was Lost Springs Canyon.

Uneasiness prickled down Johnson's spine as he sought

out the small dark gash, partially hidden by foliage, that marked the cave mouth that led under the mesa.

Plug should have sent a man back to that Triangle camp to make sure, he thought. But you couldn't tell the burly Ace of Spades foreman anything. Stewart was one of those men who ran things his way, and resented outside advice.

The thread of uneasiness lay like undigested food in Johnson as he rode into camp and dismounted.

Most of the boys were asleep in the shade. Plug was playing pinochle with Nesbit, a small, dour-faced man with the small bright eyes of a ferret. Samovar, the man who had taken a load of buckshot in his side, lay just beyond, mumbling feverishly.

Johnson led his bay into the clearing past the oaks where the other animals were tethered, Indian-style, to a rope stretched between two trees. He unsaddled, and came back toward the fire, lugging his saddle and blankets.

Plug looked up as Johnson dropped his saddle and blankets on the other side of the brush fire. "See anythin'?"

Johnson shook his head. He turned to watch a cow scramble up the bank across the stream. "Not much beef on 'em, Plug. Wish we could keep them here a week before drivin' 'em north. Get some meat on 'em."

"They're a lean lot," the burly foreman agreed. "That trek from Texas sure tells on 'em." He watched Johnson squat by the fire, rinse out a tin cup with water from his canteen and pour coffee into it from the pot setting on a flat, hot stone.

"We won't have time to change brands here," he added, scowling. "Murdock'll have to take 'em without askin' too many questions."

Johnson shrugged. "He never asked questions before—no reason to start now." He sipped the coffee.

Plug frowned. He had no love for the lanky man squatting across the fire, but Johnson was close to Allison and carried authority because of that fact.

"When you leavin' us?" he growled.

"In the mornin'. I been ridin' since I left Douglas three days ago an' my bottom side is saddle-galled. I'm turnin' in after this cup."

"Then you'll take Samovar with you," Plug said, glad to saddle Johnson with a distasteful job. 'We can't leave him here, an' he's hurt too bad to ride with us."

Johnson's lips tightened, sensing the motive behind Plug's order. Resentment crawled up in him, but he choked it back before it showed in his face.

"Sure," he said. He washed out the cup and set it down

near the pot. Plug turned back to the pinochle game, and Johnson made himself a smoke.

When it was a butt burning close to his lips he threw it into the fire, and walked to where he had dropped his saddle. He pushed it up against the tree trunk, spread his blanket out so that the saddle would pillow him, and unbuckled his gun belt.

He couldn't rid himself of a feeling that something was wrong somewhere. He knew he wouldn't sleep well. He put his feeling into words.

"Be a good idea to send a man back to that Triangle camp, Plug. Some of those Texans might be still on their feet."

Plug turned his head. "I told you we wiped 'em out—all of them." He sneered. "Yore nerves are goin' bad, Johnson. Better leave the corn likker alone."

Johnson shrugged. He had been on the cliff, taking care of the Triangle lookout, where Plug and the others raided the Triangle camp, and he had to take Plug's word for what had happened there.

He took off his boots, placed them beside the blankets, and stretched himself out. It was cool under the oak. Sunlight filtered through in tiny patches. He turned his face away from the fire, and because he was dog tired, he fell asleep instantly.

Nesbit turned over a card, tossed it on the blanket and got to his feet. "Damn," he said, clipping his word. He talked in a swift, jerky manner. "He's got me feelin' fidgety, Plug. Mebbe I better ride around."

Plug scowled. "You want to make the trip back to that Triangle Camp."

"I'd feel easier," Nesbit admitted. "Won't take me long." He glanced up at the sun almost directly overhead. "I'll be back by sundown."

The foreman reached for his sack of Bull Durham. "Yo're a damn fool!" he said testily. "But go ahead if you want."

He watched Nesbit walk to the horses, saddle a big gray, and ride off. Then he slapped viciously at the deck in front of him, scattering the cards over the blanket, and got to his feet.

Samovar called for water. He called a half-dozen times before Plug tossed his cigarette angrily away and walked to the wounded man. . . .

"Parson" Johnny lay on his stomach, surveying the rustler camp below. The sun burned against his neck and shoulders and sweat made little beads on his brown forehead and trickled into his eyes.

He had come a long way on foot, driven by hate and curiosity to see where the raiders drove the Triangle herd. He had not noticed the miles, but now, as he lay on his stomach on the slab of hot rock, he felt weariness slip into his muscles.

He wiped sweat from his eyes, and pushed a strand of damp black hair from his forehead. Heat waves shimmered between him and the rustler camp, but he could see quite clearly details about the fire.

A rider came into view around an up-river bend, heading for the camp. The kid watched him dismount and head his animal away from the fire. Later he came into sight again, walking and hunkering down by the blaze.

Johnny's attention shifted to the Triangle herd, scattered along the river. Evidently the raiders had decided to lay up there before pushing across the lava stretch beyond the valley. They acted like men with time on their hands and, Johnny thought bitterly, they had reason.

There had been a grim finality in the burst of gunfire that had swept the Triangle camp. Caught away from the others, the kid had not had time to join in the fight, and it had ended while he crouched, surprise and fear knotting his belly, in the shadows by the spring.

He did not know if any of his trailmates were still alive, for he had not gone back to see. Now, as he lay there, he felt the sharp edge of his helplessness.

It would take him at least a day to get to Douglas and break the news to Larry. It would take more time to raise a posse. Strangers did not take easily to saddle in quest of someone else's cows.

Cynicism came naturally to the solemn-faced Triangle rider, for a bitter childhood had shaped him. Orphaned before he was five, he had been kicked around by relatives with too many mouths of their own to feed. At fourteen, stunted in body, old of face, and bitter in soul, he had ridden into the Triangle yard and met with the first show of kindness since his father had died.

The passing years had eased some of his bitterness, but not his cynicism. He kept aloof from his bunkmates, content with his own company, and the feeling of being his own man under the stars. The Triangle had given him that, and in return he had given it his loyalty. And it was this loyalty that was in him now, making him fret because of his helplessness.

There was nothing he could do. He felt the press of his

Smith & Wesson .44 against his leg and he discarded the sudden thought hate had brought into him. A rifle would have given him reach into that rustler camp, but even a rifle would not have sufficed to even the score. It would take more than one gun to do that ... more guns than were left to the Triangle men who had come up the trail from Texas. ...

He squirmed back from the ledge until he was out of sight of the camp on the river. Then he got up, kept to a crouch, and ran back along the ridge until it shelved off against the mesa wall.

Twenty minutes later he paused on the bank of the stream in front of the cave. He saw Nesbit ride around the bend less than a quarter of a mile away, headed in his direction.

The brush fringing the stream hid Johnny as he slid down into the shallow water and went splashing towards the dark crevice in the mesa wall.

The coolness inside the cavern was an abrupt change from the oven heat outside, chilling the sweat on the running Triangle man. Fifty feet inside the high, rocky chamber the stream made a fifteen-foot drop into a narrow, rocky bed that angled off into the darkness. The fall boomed against the confining walls, filling the high arched room with its sound.

Johnny swung onto the wide ledge that paralleled the stream into the darkness. Farther on, Johnny remembered, the ledge parted from the stream, becoming a dark, wide passageway breaking into several other large "cave rooms" before emerging into Lost Springs Canyon.

He stumbled over slick, damp rocks, keeping away from the river now rushing through the inky blackness more than fifteen feet below him. The cavern entrance was five hundred feet behind him when he paused and looked back.

The rider was just entering the cave. Horse and man were a black etching against the sharp whiteness of the cavern mouth. The kid backed against the slick wet wall, and drew his .44. He felt the chill of the rock against his back, and a sharp, nervous excitement knotted his insides.

The booming fall would smother the shot, as it was absorbing the sound of iron-shod hoofs on the rocky floor. With the blackness of the cave wall against his back, Johnny knew he could remain unseen until the rider was on top of him. ...

Dark fluttery wings suddenly beat close to his face. Johnny twisted involuntarily, flailing with his gun at the big bat who had swooped down to investigate his presence.

Nesbit cursed as he pivoted the gray. He was less than twenty-five feet away, limned against the whiteness of the cave mouth, when Johnny fired. Nesbit tipped forward over the horn. The gray slipped it its fright, and the wiry rustler slid out of the saddle, his left arm entangled in his reins.

Johnny ran to the gray being held by its dead rider. He slipped the leather free of Nesbit's limp arm, wound it about his wrist and, bending, tugged and rolled the rustler off the ledge.

The body made a faint splash. Johnny stared down into the blackness, his gorge suddenly rising. It was the first time he had killed a man.

The gray tugged at the reins. He still felt sick as he got his foot into the stirrup and swung into saddle. . . .

Chapter 19

Six Guns Turn The Table

Hank came back to the chuck wagon where Chuck and Jim lay in the wagon's shade. Chuck, not so badly hurt as Jim, was brushing flies from Jim's beard-stubbled face. He handed Chuck a canteen he had refilled at the spring, and used his red neckerchief to wipe sweat from his eyes.

"Covered Carp an' Red," he said, kneeling beside the unconscious Jim. "Covered 'em with a tarp. Can't use a shovel, or I'da buried 'em."

Chuck nodded grimly, and Hank looked up-canyon where the red walls of the mesa loomed against the cobalt sky. "Damn 'em!" he swore helplessly.

Chuck shifted, easing his back against the wagon's rear wheel. Despite Hank's care, his shoulder was beginning to throb, as if a fever raged in it.

He gritted his teeth. "Larry should be showin' up 'bout this time—if Duke made it tuh town all right."

Hank shrugged. He got up as Jim groaned, went to the back of the wagon and found a clean neckerchief. He came back, poured water from the canteen over the neckerchief until it was soaked, then wiped Jim's cracked lips with it.

The Triangle horses, scattered during last night's raid, had drifted back to the graze and shade along the springs. The air was hot and the silence heavy in the canyon.

Chuck said: "Reckon they got Beefy—"

Hank let the bitter statement hang. After a while he got up, stretching his cramped legs. "We'll wait until mornin' for Duke an' Larry. If they don't show up I'll hitch up the wagon an' get you an' Jim inside. Mebbe I should have done it before. No use stayin' here...."

"Johnny!" Chuck muttered. "Damn it, Hank—where's the kid?"

The Triangle cook shook his head. "All I found was the cayuse he rode last night. It was saddled an' grazing with the others. No blood on the saddle, no sign of him anywhere—"

He was squinting toward the canyon entrance as he talked. He turned, relief cracking the grimness of his face. "Here's Brennan now an' Duke—"

Chuck hitched himself up to see. "Looks like they brought help...."

Brennan slid out of saddle and walked to the wagon. He said: "Hello, Chuck." Then he knelt by Jim and his face went hard.

Hank said: "Reckon Duke told you what happened?"

Brennan nodded. Hank looked back at the others. The Tumbling H men remained in saddle. Doctor Stillwell was climbing stiffly from the saddle. He reached up and untied his black bag from behind the saddle rim and turned toward the wagon. Duke and Lennie rode up and dismounted.

The medico glanced professionally at Jim's bloodied shirt front and said briskly: "I'm going to need hot water—and help." He looked at Lennie.

The girl nodded. "Whatever you say, Doctor." She began to roll up her sleeves.

Brennan went back to his horse. Hank followed him, glancing curiously at the Tumbling H riders. "It's a cold trail," he said, waving up-canyon. "But damn 'em, they drove 'em somewhere!"

Brennan nodded. "Where's Johnny?"

Hank shook his head. "Found his saddled hoss this mornin', after Duke left, but no sign of the kid." He watched Brennan get into saddle.

Bill Tate spurred his animal close to Brennan's. "Those cows of yourn left tracks," he growled. "Let's find out where they went."

Brennan nodded. Before he turned he caught the picture of Lennie, coming from the spring with a small bucket of water. She stopped and looked at him, and he kept that picture with him as he swung the black away from the wagon.

The tracks went up-canyon, swinging around a bend and ignoring the first angling break to the west. The earth underfoot became rocky, the vegetation thinning out to spiky clumps that clung close to the towering walls. The sun leaned briefly on the western wall, then slid down out of sight. The shadows leaped across the canyon floor.

Ahead of them the red mesa lifted like a giant barrier, battlemented and scoured by the winds, rain and sun of a million years. The canyon narrowed. A tongue of red rock thrust like the sharp prow of a colossal ship into the canyon, splitting it into narrow gorges.

The tracks swung right, away from the main canyon floor, threading through what became a defile in the hemming cliffs. Single file the trackers rode through this cut, to emerge in what seemed a blind pocket, completely bottled by towering walls.

Brennan reined in, frowning. Tate pulled alongside, shifting his chew to his left cheek. "Reckon this is it," he growled. "Where in hell'd they go from here? Cows can't fly!"

Daylight was leaving the pocket, being replaced by a gray, chill dusk.

Brennan said: "They drove 'em somewhere, Bill. They came in here with that Triangle herd, an' they didn't come out."

Duke interrupted, waving his good arm. "The kid! It's Parson Johnny!"

The kid was riding out of the brush choking the far wall of the pocket. He saw Brennan and suddenly hallooed, spurring his mount forward.

He pulled up, tired but excited, his brown face eager. "Through the cliffs, Larry! Other side of that wall! Our cows!"

"Take it easy, Johnny," Brennan said. Then he smiled at Johnny's excited face, feeling relief ease some of the grim tension in him. "Where have you been?"

Johnny told them. He looked at Duke when he finished. "I thought you were dead," he said. "How're the others?"

"Carp, Red and Beefy are dead," Duke told him. "Jim's hurt bad, and Chuck and Hank have lead in them."

Johnny sobered. He looked at the hard faces of the Tumbling H riders bunched around him. "We can make them pay," he said slowly.

"How many of the polecats in that valley, kid?" asked Tate.

"I counted eleven."

The Tumbling H foreman glanced around him. "Ten of us, countin' Duke—" He looked at the slim Triangle puncher with the bandaged arm.

Duke said grimly: "Count me in on this. I can still use a gun."

110

"They won't be expectin' us," Brennan said softly, staring toward the cliff that intervened between them and the rustler camp. "Mebbe we can turn the tables on them." He turned to the kid. "Lead the way, Johnny."

The moon came up over the broken hills, paling the yellow stars that speckled the sable night. It caught the shadowy figures that rode out of the cavern mouth, holding them briefly before they vanished into the velvet shadows along the river. . . .

The Ace of Spades campfire was a flickering red eye against the night. A half-dozen men were playing poker around a blanket, squinting at their cards in the firelight. Several others were sprawled around in the flame glow. Samovar was sleeping.

Johnson paced restlessly before the fire, his long shadow wavering across the men playing poker.

Plug slammed his hand into the discards and turned to him. "It's hard enough to see what I'm holdin', without you prowlin' around in front of the fire. Damn it. Ira—sit down!"

Johnson paused, feeling the rasping enmity in the burly foreman. Firelight reddened the side of his bony face. He felt the heat of it mix with the quick flare of his anger and he turned away, the shadows hiding the swift glitter in his eyes.

He walked past Samovar, the thick shadows under the oaks hiding him. The horses shifted restlessly at his approach. He paused by the side of a thick-chested sorrel, sliding a reassuring hand along the animal's flank.

"Damned jughead!" he thought feelingly. "If it wasn't for me knowin' this country he'da lost himself a long time ago." Standing there, he choked his anger back, knowing this was not the time nor the place to have it out with Plug.

A cool wind rustled among the leaves. Johnson let his thoughts ride ahead of him, back to Douglas, and what he was going to tell Allison.

His restlessness returned as he stood there, staring into the shadows by the river. After a while he went back, pausing on the edge of the fire to watch the players.

"Nesbit's takin' his time gettin' back, Plug." His uneasiness was in his voice.

Plug looked up. He was holding aces, his first good hand since he had sat down, and he didn't like Johnson's interruption. "Hell with Nesbit!" he snarled. "I'm not his guardian. Mebbe the damn fool slipped off a ledge in that cave. . . ."

One of the players guffawed. Ira stiffened.

111

"Just the same," he said, "I don't like it. Think I'll saddle up an' ride around."

Plug turned back to his game. "Watch out for the night air," he said contemptuously over his shoulder.

Johnson checked his reply. Too many easy raids had dulled the sharp edge of danger for these Ace of Spades hands. But the hunch that something was wrong was strong in the old government scout. It was an indefinable feeling, nagging at his nerves.

He turned away from the fire and went back to the tethered horses. Saddling the sorrel, he mounted and swung away from camp. He rode west, thereby missing the men that came silently, on foot, from the north and began to spread out in the darkness beyond the flickering fire. . . .

Plug raked in his winnings. "Some day I'm gonná have it out with that jasper," he said harshly, looking into the shadows where Johnson had vanished. "Tryin' to give me orders! Tellin' me what to do! *Damn him, I run this outfit!*"

No one disputed him. The game continued, with occasional curses from men who drew lousy hands. Samovar awoke and called for water. One of the kibitzers went to him and held a canteen for him to drink from.

The fire flickered down. Plug picked up his cards squinted at his hand, and cursed. "Someone rustle some wood for that fire! I can't see if I'm holdin' a jack or a lady with this pair of treys. . . ."

Monk shrugged and got up. He was a squat man with a cast in his left eye. He walked a few yards past the fire in the direction of the river and bent to gather up some dry branches that lay around the base of a gnarled oak.

He saw the shadow move against the moonlit stream. He straightened, dropping a hand to his Colt. "Nesbit!" he called sharply. "That you, Nesbit?"

A red flare answered him. The slug spun him around. He clawed his gun out of holster and fired into the dirt at his feet as the second slug from the river smashed into him, dropping him.

Cards scattered wildly across the blanket as the men around it scrambled cursingly to their feet. Lead slashed at them from the surrounding darkness. One of the rustlers crumpled across the blanket, another made a jump for the darkness beyond the fire. He was hit in midair and fell limply into the blaze, scattering the burning wood. The flame light became a small, uncertain thing against the darkness under the trees. Over it drifted the acrid smell of burning flesh. . . .

Plug made a break for the river. He stumbled over Monk's body and went sprawling. It saved him from immediate death.

Brennan swore as he overshot the burly rustler, shot again at Plug's rolling, indistinct figure, then began to run toward him. Plug scrambled to his feet and flung a shot at the Texan.

The bullet gouged across Larry's knuckles, tearing the Colt from his hand. Brennan kept running. He ploughed into the burly rustler, driving his shoulder into Plug's stomach. The shock sent Plug's Colt spinning into the shadows under the oak. Larry fell on him, driving his bloodied fist into Plug's meaty face.

The rustler threshed wildly, trying to dislodge him. Larry slammed his fist into Plug's face again. His knuckles split against Plug's teeth. Pain stabbed up his arm.

Plug choked, his mouth full of teeth and blood. He got the heel of his thick hand under Brennan's chin and shoved with desperate strength.

Larry fell back and Plug twisted, chopping down with his fist. The glancing blow spilled the Texan, giving Plug a momentary respite. He saw Larry's Colt about ten feet away, glinting in a beam of moonlight filtering through the canopy of oak leaves. He made a dive for it.

Larry landed on top of him as Plug's fingers closed over the weapon. Plug squirmed around, bringing the gun up toward Larry. He got his finger in the trigger guard, and the first bullet went off between them. The orange red flare was a dazzling flash, momentarily blinding them both.

Larry's fingers groped for the gun as Plug fired again, shooting blindly. The bullet flicked cloth from Larry's shoulder. Then his fingers found Plug's wrist and he twisted it inward. At the same time his right hand flicked across the Colt's hammer, fanning it.

Plug jerked as the bullet tore into him. He made a spasmodic motion that rolled him free of Larry and a blind instinct brought him to one knee, the Colt levelling at the Texan. The click of the hammer on a spent cartridge merged into the heavy roaring in his brain, and he scarcely felt the smash of Larry's boot against his face. . . .

Larry came into the shifting firelight. One of the Tumbling H men had dragged the body from the flames and tossed brush on the scattered embers.

Tate glanced at Brennan, noting the gash across his right hand. Blood made a dark, glinting band across his knuckles.

"Two dead by the river," Brennan said shortly. He looked around and felt relief when he saw Duke and Johnny. His eyes came back to the Tumbling H foreman. "How many?"

"Countin' yore two that makes seven who'll be doin' their rustlin' in hell!" Tate growled. He motioned to a pair of sullen, disarmed men by the fire. Johnny was holding a gun on them. "These two decided to call it quits. There's a wounded galoot under that tree."

"That makes ten." Brennan frowned. "You sure you counted eleven, Johnny?"

The kid nodded. "I followed 'em all the way. Countin' the wounded one there was eleven of the skunks."

Tate spat into the flames. "Reckon one of 'em got away." He was not dissatisfied. This was the showdown for which he had waited for a long time. He was sorry Bob Masters had not been along.

"What we gonna do with these two?" Lefty asked.

"String 'em up!" Tate snapped. To him that was the only logical conclusion to the career of a brand-blotter.

Brennan shook his head. "McVail's been askin' for proof. Here's his proof, Bill."

Tate held out for a quick hanging, but he was overruled by the majority opinion that held with Brennan. Larry walked to Johnny. "Want to wrap my handkerchief around this, kid?" He held up his bleeding hand.

The kid obeyed. His face was white, and he looked a little sick.

Tate said: "Nichols got grazed across the ribs with a lucky shot from one of these polecats. Outside of that, an' yore hand, Brennan, we didn't get a scratch."

Larry looked into the flames. The picture of Lennie came back to him. Tall and slender, sleeves rolled back, stopping to look at him. The fading sun had been behind her, shadowing her features, and the clear beauty of that picture danced and faded in the crackling fire.

"We'll wait until daylight before drivin' the cows back," he said, turning toward Tate. "That cave passage is too tricky to try at night. . . ."

Lennie saw the cattle come around the canyon bend and the heaviness that had been with her all night ran out of her. She stood up and waited, feeling her heart pound at sight of the big man who swung his horse away from the herd to ride toward the wagon.

"All accounted for," Larry said. "Nobody hurt." He waved his hand toward the cattle. "You'll have them grazin' on Tumblin' H grass before night."

The cattle were not on Lennie's mind. "Your hand," she said. "You're hurt."

114

Larry shrugged. The doctor came toward them. "I'll have a look at it," he said. He paused to watch the herd string past, headed for the canyon mouth.

Tate rode over as the doc cleaned and bandaged the gash on Larry's hand. He saw the way Lennnie was looking at Larry and he nodded to himself.

The Texan would be good for her. She had been too much alone, and too concerned with her brother. It would be good for her to have a man take over some of her responsibility.

"We ought to make Tumblin' H grass in seven hours, pushin' 'em," he said. "We can scatter 'em just past the North Fork ridges. Time enough to cut out an' rebrand after we settle things in Douglas."

Brennan said: "Go ahead, Bill. I'll stay with the wagon, give the doc a hand with Chuck an' Jim. . . ."

Hank had already hitched the team to the wagon. Chuck and Jim were carefully carried inside. The doc climbed up beside Hank on the seat, after tying his saddle hoss behind the wagon.

"See you in town," he waved to Lennie and Brennan. "Go ahead—we'll make it all right."

Brennan and the girl turned away and spurred after the Triangle herd filing through the canyon mouth. . . .

Chapter 20

Jail Break

Allison poured himself another drink. He turned and caught Barney looking at him and his lips tightened tensely.

The sun was westerning. Masters would be showing up pretty soon, unless the sheriff was running a bluff. But Allison knew Masters hadn't been bluffing.

The gambler shook off his impatience. Let the law come! He wasn't going to pull out of Timberlake now, not when he held control of the wide valley in the palm of his hand.

He turned, picking out his men among the scattered customers at the tables. Eight, including Crawford and Gans. More than enough to stop Masters and Albright. . . .

He took a cigar from his vest pocket and lighted it. He moved his shoulders, feeling the hardness of his shoulder holster and gaining reassurance from it. It had been a long time since he had killed a man, but the feeling was not new to him, and as he turned to pour himself another drink he felt the impatience go out of him, leaving him cold and expectant.

The swinging doors creaked on their hinges. Allison turned his head, his hand lifting to the front of his coat in a swift, instinctive gesture. Then it fell away and a scowl darkened his face.

Carsons paused just inside the room, swinging his head around in a quick survey. He saw Charley and came walking toward the bar, talking as he came. "I want to see you, Charley. Upstairs—in your office!"

The gambler shrugged, a thin curl of contempt twisting his lips. Carsons was going to pieces, just waiting.

He took his bottle and glass from the bar and went upstairs, Carsons silent now as he followed. He went around the desk and put the whiskey bottle and glass on the desk in front of him, then leaned back in his chair and surveyed the nervously pacing banker.

"Damn it, Mark—sit down!" he snapped.

The banker ignored the order. He paused and looked at Allison, his face gray, almost the color of his goatee. "What are you going to do Charley?"

"Nothing!" the gambler snapped. "I'm going to let Mc-Vail make the moves. I told you that yesterday when you ran over here."

"McVail won't back down!" Carsons bleated. "You know that, Charley—he won't back down!"

"I've got eight men downstairs," Charley reminded him coldly. "Men I hired because they could handle guns. If the law comes pushin' in here tonight there's gonna be a couple of vacancies in that department in the morning."

Carsons shook his head. He had sought power ever since coming to Timberlake Valley—sought it for its own sake. It had never been enough. He had never let anything stand in his way, not even friendship. When he'd found out the Kansas Pacific was building west through Timberlake he had decided he wanted the Tumbling H. He'd make a deal with Allison to break Halliday, thinking he could remain safely in the background if anything went wrong.

Time—and the law—had finally caught up with him. The arrogance based on the unstable foundation of his power had tottered with its collapse. He had but one thought now, to try to save himself from the dishonor that was soon to come to him and his family.

"It'll backfire," he said bitterly. "The whole thing. Yo' can't shoot the law without some kind of an investigation from outside."

Charley got up, breaking coldly into the banker's state-

116

ment. "Shut up, and do what I tell you. Let me handle McVail and Albright. And tomorrow you take care of that Tumbling H loan, call it in. Don't forget, those surveyors will be here in another two weeks."

Carsons' head bowed. "I should never have gotten mixed up with you."

"It's too late to start getting religion," Charley sneered. "You get back to the bank and sit it out. We'll handle the law when it comes around tonight."

He sat back, chewing on his cigar, after Carsons left. After a while he got up and went out to the balcony. . . .

Johnson came in, slamming the batwings against the wall. The lanky killer carried trouble with him. Charley sensed it by the way Johnson crossed the room to the bar with long strides, saw it in the dust and sweat that stuck to the man, and heard it in Johnson's raspy voice as he faced Barney across the bar.

"Where's Charley?"

"Up here!" Allison called, while Barney was opening his mouth.

Johnson whirled and headed for the stairs. Crawford and Gans, who were at the bar, turned to look after Johnson, and Allison caught their eye and motioned them to follow.

They eased into Allison's office behind Johnson, closing the door behind them. Allison whirled on the lanky gunman. "What happened, Ira—what's gone wrong?"

"Everythin'!" the killer snapped. "Damn it, everythin's gone wrong, Charley. Just because that jughead segundo of yores got careless—"

"What happened?"

Johnson caught himself and forced his anger back. "Wiped out," he said harshly. "Plug—an' the rest of the boys, except Samovar, Kelly an' Cantwell. I saw them when I slipped back, after the firin' stopped."

Allison's face corded. "Damn it, Johnson!—start from the beginning. What happened at Lost Springs?"

Johnson told him, leaving out no details, sprinkling his narrative with contempt for Plug. "I don't know what happened to Nesbit," he concluded. "Probably ran into Brennan an' the Tumblin' H men." He paused, his teeth showing against flattened lips.

"I couldn't believe it, Charley! Brennan! I saw him drop—"

"It was Brennan all right," Allison gritted. "He came to town the same night you showed up at the ranch, and killed Saber. McVail jailed him for the night and let him out next morning. Around noon a Triangle puncher showed

117

up and about an hour later the Tumbling H pulled out with them."

Johnson said: "They'll be comin' to town...."

Allison whirled on him. "Let 'em come. I'm not running!" He looked at Gans and Crawford. "There's almost a dozen of us here, counting Barney. We'll stop Brennan, and what's left of the Tumbling H right here—in the Casino!"

Johnson nodded. "I could have kept goin'—cleared the country, Charley. But I knew Brennan would be comin' to town, an' I wanted to be here when he came!"

Crawford looked at Gans. The Laredo gunster shrugged. "We'll be downstairs, Charley." His voice was noncommital. They went out.

Allison's lips curled. He knew their kind. They stuck by a man who hired them as long as they saw him ahead of the game, as long as he could pay....

Gans and Crawford went out through the back door to the shed behind the Casino and saddled horses. They rode out through the alley to the street and turned south. They rode unhurriedly. At the bank they dismounted, dropped reins over the hitchrail, and turned toward the door.

Vanity Carsons came out of the bank as they paused on the walk. Crawford and Gans both looked after her as she passed. Crawford said: "Pretty trick." He grinned crookedly. "Too bad we can't take her with us."

They opened the door and stepped inside. There were no other customers in the bank. The cashier was in his cage, totaling receipts for the day. Crawford stayed by the door. Gans walked unhurriedly to the window.

The Laredo gunman took his Colt out of holster and laid the barrel on the shelf of the pay window. He said quietly: "Pass over everythin' you have, bud. Don't make a fuss an' you won't get hurt."

The clerk stiffened. His eyes left Gans for Crawford. Crawford was sliding the bolt back on the door. Then he walked to the windows and started pulling down the shades. It was past closing time and the move, seen from outside, would arouse no curiosity.

The clerk began stuffing specie and bills into a small canvas sack. Gans glanced at the clock over the door. "Hurry it up!" he snapped.

Behind the low mahogany railing to the left of the cashier's cage was a door with a sign lettered in gold paint: *Mark Carsons*—Private.

The banker was behind that door, slumped at his desk. Vanity had just been in to see him. She had been unusual-

118

ly affectionate, and he was glad she would be leaving on the morning stage for Virginia.

He heard the scrape of booted feet in the room outside his office and then the sound of the shades being pulled down. He glanced at his heavy gold watch. Four-thirty. Tom was closing up.

Carsons pushed back in his chair and got up. He walked heavily to the door, opened it, and came out into the small space behind the railing. . . .

Gans whirled and fired. The move was reflexive. Carsons staggered, an amazed expression on his face. Gans shot again, his lips curling in an animal snarl. Carsons seemed to trip over an invisible barrier; he fell against the railing and slid down.

Gans reached inside the cashier's cage and jerked the canvas sack from the clerk's nerveless fingers. He shot the fear-paralyzed clerk before turning away . . . shot him out of pure viciousness.

Crawford had the door open. Gans ran across the room and followed him into the street. . . .

Jim Masters and Ben Albright left Kenny in the law office and went down the walk. They met Vanity on the corner. The sheriff tipped his hat. "Good afternoon, Vanity."

She nodded, giving him a tremulous smile. She was dressed for traveling and she was carrying a small bag.

"Your father still at the bank?"

"Yes." She was impatient and nervous and Albright turned to look after her.

"Think she's goin' in to see the kid, Jim?"

The sheriff shrugged. "She's leaving in the morning—going East. Might be she wants to say good-bye to Bob."

They went up the street, crossed over to Main, and paused on the walk across from the bank. Ben squinted at the building. "Shades are down," he said laconically. "Looks like Carsons closed up an' went home."

"Sometimes he stays behind, in his office," Masters said. "Let's take a look."

The shots were muffled behind the closed doors, but they reached across the street like a warning bell. Albright said: "What the hell—" Then deputy and sheriff pivoted as one and headed across the street.

There was another shot just as the door swung open. Crawford appeared on the walk, gun in hand. He slammed a shot at the sheriff and made a run for one of the horses at the rail. He got a foot in the stirrup and was lifting himself into the saddle when Masters' shot stiffened him. He slid down between the hoofs of the frightened animal.

Gans came jumping out, his gun spitting. The sheriff stumbled as a bullet gashed his right leg. He went down, shooting high, smashing a window in the bank behind Gans.

Albright spun around and sat down. Crawford was trying to get to his feet. Gans made a flying leap over him, still holding the canvas bag in his left hand. He got into saddle and Albright's shot killed the animal under him.

Gans rolled free. He whirled, and made a jump for the other bronc. The frightened animal was breaking away from the rail, its reins trailing. Gans hit saddle and flattened himself along the animal's neck. He made a bad target and the sheriff missed.

Masters started to limp after the rider. Albright sat in the middle of the street. He couldn't get up. He saw Crawford move. The outlaw was lifting his Colt, lining it on the running sheriff.

Albright steadied his muzzle with his left hand and pulled the trigger. Crawford slumped into the dust without firing.

It was over before the men, spilling out into the street, realized what had happened. They grouped around Albright, and stared at the sheriff as he came limping back.

"Got away," Masters gritted. "But he can't get far. My last shot hit his hoss."

A man staggered out of the bank. "McVail!" he called, sighting the sheriff. "McVail! Bank robbed—Carsons shot . . ."

Several men caught him as he fell. The rest of them were scattering for guns and horses. One of them said; "Comin', Sheriff?"

Masters shook his head. "You can run him down without me. I'm getting Ben to the doc's."

"Stillwell's out of town," the man frowned.

"I know," Masters said. "Tepple will have to do."

"That hoss doctor!" snorted the man, whirling away. . . .

Kenny cautiously slid the bolt back on the door and opened it slightly, keeping the shotgun between him and the door.

Vanity Carsons said: "I want to see Bob Masters."

Kenny frowned. "I'm sorry, Miss Carsons—"

"Please!" the girl said. "I'll only be a few minutes. I'm leaving town early tomorrow morning. I'm going East. I want to say good-bye."

Kenny hesitated. McVail had left orders to let no one in while he and Albright were gone. But the bucktoothed man

120

saw no harm in this pale-faced girl with the shadows under her dark eyes.

"Just a few minutes, Miss Carsons," he said. He smiled as she came inside. "You look as though you are ready to travel now."

He took the keys from the hook over McVail's desk and led the way to Bob's cell. Bob was pacing around in his cubicle. He stopped when Kenny said: "Visitor for you, Masters." He looked at Vanity and a faint smile eased the harshness around his mouth.

Kenny fitted a key in the lock and turned it. "I'll wait in the corri—"

His jaw dropped and his eyes grew round. He was looking into the muzzle of a small bore pistol in the hand of Miss Carsons, and if he saw no hostility in the eyes behind it, he saw determination.

Bob came swiftly to his side and clamped a hand over the shotgun's hammer before Kenny could move. He jerked the gun from Kenny's hand and shoved him roughly inside. "Keep yore face shut!" he snarled, "or they'll find a corpse in that cell!"

He clanged the door shut and turned the key in the lock. Then he turned to the girl, standing rigidly by the bars.

"All right," he said, his voice gentler. "You can put that gun away now, Vanity."

The girl's arm went limp at her side, the stiffness left her body. "I've got the horses out in front. Across the street, so McVail wouldn't suspect anything. Hired them earlier this afternoon and brought them there." Her voice came swiftly. "We'll have to hurry—"

"No !I'm not leavin', Vanity. Not right away." The youngster started as shots broke out north of the jail. Then he swung around, poking the muzzle of the shotgun through the bars. "Where's McVail?" he asked harshly. "Where is he, Kenny?"

The savagery in the kid's face had shaken better men than the bucktoothed temporary deputy. He had heard stories and he knew that Masters would kill when he was that way. He wet his lips. "Gone to the Casino—to see Allison—"

Masters sneered. He turned and strode into the law office, ignoring the white-faced girl in the corridor. He tossed the shotgun and the keys on the cot and began to pull out drawers in the sheriff's desk. He found his gun and belt in one of them.

Vanity came into the room as he was buckling the heavy belt around his waist. "Bob!" She caught his arm as he started to swing away. "If we leave now we'll have our

121

chance at happiness! Don't let me down now! I did this for you—for us. I know you didn't kill your uncle. I want to ride with you—live with you—somewhere far from here. Isn't that what you wanted—"

He shook off her hand. He was past listening to her, to anyone. He had paced that narrow cell with one thought growing, clamoring in his mind. *Kill McVail!*

She caught him at the door, wedging her body between him and the hard wood. "If you leave me now, Bob—we're through! You hear that? Through!"

She was a slip of a girl, fighting for what she wanted. She had been a shy, moody girl most of her life, kept in subjection by her arrogant sire. But she had rebelled when he had ordered her to quit seeing Bob. And now her slim body was tensed, her dark eyes afire with bitter challenge.

Her intensity stopped Bob. He looked down into her face, knowing that he wanted her, had always wanted her since the day he had come riding back from beyond the Diamond Heads, a wild button on a dusty sorrel, and had seen her sitting saddle on the rim of the desert, alone and girlishly wondering, watching the setting sun paint the mesas deep purple.

Her love of solitude, her quiet delight in the beauty of the desert, her quick eagerness which revealed itself to him as they talked had kindled a fellow feeling in Bob. And in the two years that had followed—despite the stern disapproval of the elder Carsons—they had seen much of each other.

He didn't want to lose her. Yet that deadly rage inside him, that devil that paced in his blood, brushed aside her plea. He bent and gathered her in his arms and kissed her. All this restlessness, his wildness, was in that kiss. Then he lifted her out of his way and stepped out.

He had sworn to kill McVail when he got out—and nothing short of death would stop him now....

Chapter 21

The Reckoning

Vanity stood in the doorway. Inside the jail Kenny was beginning to yelp for help. The girl slumped against the framing, her mind numb, not caring any more what happened. She didn't hear Sam's voice until he ran across the street and shook her.

"Bob Masters!" he cried. "My Gawd, girl—you didn't let him out—"

The girl nodded dully. Kenny was making a racket in the jail.

"We had it all planned," she said. "We were going away together. I thought he meant it. I believed him. But he left me—"

There was fear in Sam's voice. "Where? Where did he go?"

"To the Casino. He's gone to kill McVail!"

The shock of it grayed Sam's face. "No! Good Lawd, girl—he can't do that! *McVail's his father!*"

The girl looked up into his contorted face, not comprehending. Sam pushed past her. He found the jail keys on the cot and ran into the corridor.

Kenny was at the door, yelling. He stopped when he saw Sam. "That girl!" he grumbled. "She held a gun on me."

"Never mind that!" Sam muttered. "We've got to stop that wild kid. Stop him before he makes the biggest mistake of his hot-headed life!"

"What happened?" Kenny growled. "I heard shots. . . ."

"Crawford and Gans robbed the bank. They shot Carsons and young Tom Blaine. Albright and the sheriff shot it out with them. Albright was wounded, badly. Crawford never got into saddle. But Gans made it out of town, with a posse right behind him."

"Where's the sheriff?"

"Gone to the Casino," Sam said. He had the door open, swinging it wide. "Come on!" he said harshly. "We've got to round up help. Someone's got to back McVail up!"

Vanity was standing in the doorway, staring at him as he turned. He brushed past her, reached into the wall rack for a rifle. Kenny picked up the shotgun Bob had tossed on the cot.

Vanity took hold of Sam's arm as he made for the door. "My father!" she said, choking over her words. "I heard you tell Kenny my father was shot!"

"Yes," Sam said, pitying her. "Shot pretty badly, Vanity. Doc Tepple doesn't think he'll live."

The girl stood stricken as they left. Then she followed, began to run toward the bank.

Brennan reined to a halt on a rise in the river trail. Lennie was at his side. The others crowded around.

"Looks like trouble," the big Texan said, pointing down toward Douglas. "There's a posse raisin' dust out of town or I need glasses!"

Lennie turned a white face toward him. "It can't be Bob!

He couldn't have—" She turned to watch, dread tightening her lips.

Whoever the rider ahead of that posse was, he was too far away to be recognized. They were small motes raising dust on the winding trail that led up past Hurricane Ledge.

Tate pushed up alongside Brennan. "We better get down there and find out what's happened. Mebbe Bob did get out."

They swept down in Douglas. Socrates Sam and Kenny were cutting across the street as Brennan drew up in front of the bank where a small group of older men and women and wide-eyed children were looking at Crawford's body, still lying in the street.

Sam yelled: "Brennan! The kid's on the loose!" He came running up, winded and a little incoherent. "Bob's gone after McVail. Stop him, Brennan! The young fool doesn't know McVail's his father!"

Brennan looked down at Sam. "What are you gettin' at—"

"Go on—stop him!" the oldster yelled. "I'll explain it later. There's no time now, Brennan. Stop the kid from killin' McVail. The sheriff is Jim Masters, Bob's father!"

"Where?" Brennan snapped. "Where's McVail?"

"In the Casino. Gone for a showdown with Allison."

Brennan pivoted his weary mount. Tate crowded him. "I heard Sam!" the Tumbling H foreman said. "If McVail's gone gunnin' for Allison, I want to be in on it."

Lennie looked down at Sam, the shock of his words holding her. "Sam—what are you saying? What's happened?"

"Vanity got your brother out of jail," Sam said. "Bob left her to go to the Casino—to kill McVail. But McVail's your father."

The girl came out of saddle, lithe as a tigress. "Sam! *How do you know?*"

"I've known for a long time," Sam said. "Ever since McVail dropped his watch at my place, one night, after helping to bring in a body. There was a small copy of that family picture you have back at the ranch inside his watch case. He told me the whole story later. . . . How he deserted your mother." Sam's voice softened at the look on Lennie's face. "He made no excuses, Lennie. He wanted nothing, except to stay here in Timberlake Valley as Jim McVail, where he could see you and Bob occasionally. That's all he wanted—"

The shots that broke out in the Casino, far down the street, were like periods falling into place, ending the story of Jim Masters—alias Sheriff Jim McVail.

Sam turned. Brennan and the Tumbling H riders were

124

just swinging in toward the Casino rails. "Looks like it's too late," he said, and began to walk down the street toward the sounds of gunfire.

Allison was waiting with his back against the long bar when McVail thrust aside the batwing doors and limped in.

The sheriff paused, sliding his steely glance about the big gaming room, picking out the men scattered at tables and under the balcony. Allison had called him, fortifying his hand with hired guns. But Allison was going to die before the sun set. The knowledge was in Jim Masters as he stood there, sensing the trap Allison had set. No one in that gambling hall could stop him from doing that.

This was the end of it, the long, bitter road Masters had traveled since he had gone back to Memphis to find his family gone. He had come drifting into the Timberlake, a silent, scarred man, unrecognized and lonely and empty inside. He made no excuses to himself, nor to anyone else, for having deserted his wife. He had been restless and too demanding—she had been frail and cold—and he had lived with her as long as he could.

He had found the woman he could have loved. She had been an entertainer on the "Missouri Queen"—a side-wheeler making the run from St. Louis to St. Joseph. He had found her—and lost her.

He had never doubted but that Allison had had something to do with the burning of the Missouri Queen. But he was going to kill Allison for more than that.

He had waited and watched while Allison reached out for power in Timberlake valley. He had stood by while Halliday's Tumbling H was stripped and plundered, not daring to buck Allison because of what Charley knew. He had not wanted his children to find out, but Charley had finally forced his decision.

Allison sensed the finality in the scarred lawman as Masters began to walk toward the bar. He resisted the desire to glance up at the balcony, to reassure himself that Johnson was up there, in the shadows, a gun in his hand, covering the sheriff. He didn't move.

"The sun's getting red in the street," McVail said.

Allison smiled. "You didn't really think I'd leave town, did you, Jim?"

"It would have been your first smart move in a long time," McVail answered. He looked around to the men waiting ... waiting for him to move. . . .

"A couple of your men pulled out on you, Charley," he said softly. "Crawford and Gans." He saw a flicker in Alli-

125

son's eyes. "Crawford's dead. They robbed the bank on their way out. Gans will be swinging from the end of a rope inside of an hour."

Allison shrugged. "That was Gans' mistake, not mine. I'm going to be here a long time, Jim—a long time after you're gone!"

The light was fading against the windows.

"One thing, Charley," the sheriff said, as if making a last request. "You killed Diamond Kate, didn't you?"

Charley's eyes met the sheriff's. "I knew her first, Jim. And then you came—cutting me out. She threw me over for you, and no woman could do that—"

The slamming of the batwings made a harsh sound that dribbled off into the powder-keg stillness.

Bob Masters paced into the room and wheeled to face his father!

It was Ira Johnson who stopped the kid from killing Jim Masters. He did it unintentionally. Waiting in the shadows on the balcony, he was tensed for a move from the sheriff that would be his signal to shoot.

Bob's sudden entrance set off his taut nerves. He stepped out of the shadows and fired.

McVail staggered against the bar.

Young Masters pivoted and fired by reflex, his bullet splintering the rail close to Johnson, driving the lanky killer back. Allison whirled, making a run for the stairs.

The sheriff steadied himself against the bar. His voice struck out at Bob, shaping his actions. "Get him, Bob! Get Allison!"

Bob obeyed, not knowing why . . . moving to something in the sheriff's tone, some implicit faith that Bob would do his bidding. The youngster had expected to find the sheriff in close collaboration with Allison . . . and the shock of finding that he and McVail had stepped into a loaded trap brushed aside his primary purpose.

His first shot spun Charley around before the gambler reached the end of the bar. Charley turned, a gun in his hand, and received two slugs, another from young Masters and one from the sheriff. He went down, on his knees first, as if reluctant to die, and the last thing he saw was young Masters running toward the bar, and Jim Masters, grinning crookedly, thumbing the hammer of his Colt. . . .

The kid was hit before he reached the sheriff. Masters lurched away from the bar, spun Bob behind him, and emptied his Colt at the men shooting from across the room. Then he bent over Bob, shielding the youngster with his body. . . .

126

Brennan and the Tumbling H men burst into the room then. Johnson fired at the big Texan, his bullet drawing Brennan's attention. He cursed as his hammer clicked against a spent cartridge. Brennan was coming up the stairs.

He ran back into Allison's office, crossed the room to the door opening on the back stairs. A bullet from down in the yard splintered wood near his head. He jerked back and met Brennan in the doorway.

Johnson threw his useless Colt at the Texan and drew his knife. Brennan hit him before he got it free, spinning him against the wall. Johnson squirmed away as Larry closed in. He stepped back, felt the railing against his buttocks, and slipped his knife out as Larry came for him.

Larry caught his arm, twisted, and heaved. Johnson gave a sharp cry as he went over the railing.

Brennan looked over the railing at a suddenly quiet scene. Two of Allison's gunslingers were lined up against the east wall, not wanting any more of the fight. One was sitting on the floor near Johnson's broken body, holding his hand tightly against the hole in his stomach. Three others were definitely out of the fight.

He turned and came down the stairs. Bill Tate was standing beside Bob, looking down at the sheriff's body. A bullet had creased Bob's head, and the blood ran down his stubbled cheek, like a red gash in his face, making him resemble the scarred man who had stood over him, shielding him with his body.

"I came in to kill him," he was saying, "and instead I helped him kill Allison. Why, Bill?" He looked down at his father, not knowing, wondering. "Why did he do it?"

"Sam'll tell you," Brennan said, moving toward them. "It's a long story. Let's get out of here."

They buried Jim Masters on the knoll beside his wife and Jeff Halliday. Bob left them as they walked back to the ranch. He mounted his horse and rode toward town, and Brennan, standing beside Lennie, knew he was going to see Vanity Carsons.

"Carsons cleared up a lot of things before he died," said Socrates Sam, watching Bob top the rise in the river trail and vanish. "If he hadn't confessed how he killed Jeff, a lot of people might still be thinking Bob did it."

Tate grunted. "Never figgered Carsons as a killer."

Brennan looked up at Lennie. She was on the stairs, staring at the river road, and after a while she turned and caught his look.

He said. "I'll be leavin'—"

127

Her eyes held his steadily, and he saw in them what he wanted to see.

"I've got to send Barstow a wire," he said. "And I want to drop into the doc's office an' visit Chuck an' Jim. I want to see Duke an' Johnny an' Hank. I want to say good-bye."

"Good-bye?"

He nodded. "They'll be leavin' for Texas soon. But I'm stayin'—here."

He saw the gladness in Lennie's eyes as he turned away.

THE END